MASTER OF SIN

SIENNA SNOW

GODS OF VEGAS, BOOK 1

BY SIENNA SNOW

Copyright Page

Cover Design: Steamy Designs

Editor: Jennifer Haymore

www.siennasnow.com

ISBN - eBook - 978-1-948756-08-2

ISBN - Print - 978-1-948756-09-9

CHAPTER ONE

Penny

"PENNY, you need to find someone who brings out the wild side you try so hard to repress."

I stared at my younger brother, Adrian, as if he'd lost his mind.

"Don't look at me like that. I'm serious. You're twenty-seven and live like you're an eighty-year-old spinster."

"Yes, you're right. I'll get right onto dancing on tables between working sixty-hour weeks and keeping Mommy Dearest away from us."

No matter how much I wanted it, there was no way I could afford to let loose. Especially if I wanted to continue to make sure Adrian's future was protected. My passions, desires, and true nature would remain locked down behind the walls of the all-business Persephone Kipos. Any deviation from the uptight girl I projected could lead to my stepmother ousting me from the company I was so desperate to save.

"Penny, I give two shits about the company or what Mom thinks. Besides, in less than two months I will own my shares outright. Then you and I together will own the majority of the company and the woman who gave birth to me can go back to banging the pool boy."

I bit the inside of my mouth trying to hold in my thoughts on the situation of his inheritance. If Dara Trevor Kipos had any say, she would never relinquish control of the shares or the company. If my suspicions were right, her acquiring the percentage she currently owned was due to nefarious circumstances anyways.

I'd known as a seven-year-old that my stepmother only cared about Papa's money and status. She'd preyed on my father, Jacob Kipos, a lonely widower, and somehow convinced him I needed a mother. When in reality, the last thing she ever wanted to do was be a mother to me or the baby she'd conceived to force Papa's hand into marriage.

It had taken another five years before Papa had seen through Dara's manipulation and filed for divorce. Not three days later, a drunk driver had run him off the road, killing him the moment his car hit a tree.

Which in turn left Dara in charge of two minors and a billion-dollar horticulture import-export business.

Convenient how things worked out in her favor.

I knew without a doubt that she was involved in Papa's death, but I couldn't prove it. And until Adrian owned his shares outright, I'd hold off on pursuing my suspicions and play the dutiful, yet weak, Kipos heiress.

"I'll make a deal with you. The second you turn twenty-one, I will kick up my heels and party like it's 1999."

He rolled his eyes. "I'll be fifty before you do anything that would go against Mom's rules. Did you forget I know in detail what you spend your free time doing? By the way, have you decided on whether you're going wide or keeping it limited?"

My eyes nearly bugged out of their sockets as I scanned the room, making sure one of Dara's spies disguised as cleaning staff wasn't around. Besides Adrian and a few trusted people, no one knew anything about what I did outside of Kipos International.

The house Papa had bought for my mom was no longer the safe haven it had been before Dara entered the picture. Yes, I owned half of it, but because Adrian had inherited the other half, Dara had access.

And she'd placed many spies in the house masquerading as staff. Adrian and I had learned early on in life to keep all conversations about our personal business outside of any property Dara could freely enter.

It was through a listening device that she'd discovered the name of the boy I'd had a crush on as a teen. She'd used the information to embarrass me in front of his family and then told me I would never attract a boy like him. It wasn't until a few weeks after the incident that I discovered the bug while cleaning my room. After that day, I made sure never to have any conversations in the house that I wasn't okay with Dara hearing.

Even the condo Kipos had given me as part of my executive package was only used to sleep in. All of my personal and business files and property were kept safe at a warehouse I rented near my cousin Henna's house.

"Watch what you say in here. I don't want any backlash coming in your direction. Dara probably has this place bugged again."

"Oh, she does."

"What?" I shouted.

Fuck. If Dara got any inclination I had interests outside of Kipos International, she'd go out of her way to destroy them.

"Don't worry. I took care of any issues. The few things I found are now safe in the pool house with a recording of the activities of her most recent boy toy."

"You nearly gave me a heart attack." I dropped my head to the back of the couch and released a relieved breath.

"Your private activities are safe." A grin touched his lips, and he picked up the soda sitting on the coffee table next to his party-sized tray of chicken nuggets. "No one will ever find out you're a closeted freak who'd rather make love to her elderflower concoctions than a real man."

"Great, now you're a comedian."

"Penny. I'm not an idiot." His voice grew irritated. "I'm smarter than you believe. Everything's under control. No one can enter this room, moreover this property, without me knowing or having any listening device scrambled."

"How the hell would you know..." I trailed off and then said, "What the fuck are you mixed up in?"

"Do you know you only cuss when you're worried?"

"Adrian," I warned.

"You're the one who made me do those coding classes as a kid."

"Don't make me kill you." I clenched my jaw.

That was when it hit me. How else would he have been able to get me the financials of various companies for some of my proposals? I hadn't questioned him initially, but as of late I'd wondered how an almost-twenty-one-year-old was able to get confidential information on companies that was only privy to a company's inner circle.

"You're a hacker. Oh my God, I knew having tech

mogul Cristo David's son as a roommate was too good to be true." I folded my arms across my body and glared at my too-smart-for-his-own-good brother.

"Oh, shit, your foot is doing that *tap, tap, tap* thing. It's not as bad as you think." He raised his hands in surrender. "I swear there's nothing to worry about. Nearly everything I've ever done has been on the up-and-up."

"Adrian, do not get mixed up in anything that will get you in trouble. I have enough crap on my shoulders to add the possibility of you getting arrested to it."

"Too late." He popped a chicken nugget into his mouth. "College is a place to make new friends and acquaintances. Some will help me succeed by opening the right doors and others will give me the tools to run Kipos International until I find someone to do the job for me."

"And hacking's part of it? I will not have your future destroyed. Do you hear me?"

"It isn't private if the information is located on unsecured servers."

"I swear to God. You could drive a person to drink." I inhaled deeply a few times in hopes of letting it calm me enough not to strangle my baby brother. "Who are you involved with?"

He responded by picking up another nugget from the table in front of us and taking a bite of the breaded white meat.

I gave him the glare that used to make him hide when we were younger.

He held my gaze in challenge. Then after a few seconds, he sighed and looked away. "You have that death stare mastered."

I continued my irritated stance. Dara may not care what happened to Adrian, but I would do everything in my power to make sure he succeeded. He was all I had left. I would walk straight into the fires of hell to protect him.

"If you have to know, it's with the Lykaios brothers."

My heart stopped, and a wave of uneasiness settled on my shoulders.

"You've got to be kidding me. Do you have any idea what will happen if Dara finds out?" I stood and began to pace. "There has to be a way to get you out of whatever deal you made with them."

"It's not like they're mafia. Hagen, Pierce, and Zack probably know more about running a billion-dollar company than anyone else we know. Hell, each of them are masters in their fields. You'd be amazed at how much I've learned in the past year. They don't hold any punches when it comes to telling me where I fucked up, but they give me credit when I bring something new to the table."

"Past year?" My voice grew high pitched as I pinched the bridge of my nose. "Why am I finding out about this now?"

"Because I knew you'd react this way. No matter what Mom wants to think, they are legit businessmen who made a success of their lives. You're the one who told me not to take everything at face value."

I knew better than anyone the Lykaios brothers were very different than the image they projected to the world. Hell, I'd grown up with them.

Rhea Lykaios had been my mother, Karina's, best friend. They were both heiresses from Patras, a large Greek city built at the foothills of Mount Panachaikon, overlooking the Gulf of Patras. My mother was the daughter of an Indian shipping magnate who moved to Greece from India. And Rhea was the daughter of an international spice distributor. The two women had met during a school field trip and become fast friends. One of those ride-or-die things, as my mama used to say.

They'd both ended up marrying Greek businessmen who moved to Vegas. Nearly every holiday I could remember before Mama died was celebrated with the Lykaioses. I'd even for a short time believed the Lykaios boys were my brothers.

No, that wasn't true.

Pierce and Zack were like my brothers, being only a few years older than me, and in a sense still were. But Hagen. He was another story. The oldest brother was the boy every mom knew would be bad for their daughter.

He'd been the rebel, constantly in trouble and unapologetic. He'd fascinated me—especially those intense, mesmerizing eyes of his. It was as if he could see down to the depths of my soul.

He was the only man who'd ever made me want things the prim and proper Persephone Kipos should never reach toward. Good thing I'd outgrown it.

Liar.

Now he fascinated me even more. He was truly the dark, dangerous man any sane woman was supposed to keep a safe distance from but couldn't resist. He ran the majority of Vegas nightlife, from top restaurants and dance clubs to shows. Though there were rumors he was also involved in the underworld of Vegas. But deep down I knew he wasn't what everyone believed him to be.

The experiences of my childhood had disappeared once Dara came into the picture. Any visits went from running around our houses, playing games, and getting into mischief to formal events wrapped in etiquette and order. Dara had kept up the "old traditions" as she liked to call them, for a few years, but something had happened around the time I turned eleven, causing a massive fight between Rhea and Dara. All I could remember was the anger on Dara's face and the directive that we were no longer going to associate with any Lykaios.

"Penny, are you listening? They're pretty decent guys despite the rumors."

"I know this. I grew up with them. I'm just afraid of what Dara will do if she knows you work for them. I don't need my Kipos inheritance. My mom left me enough money to fund a lifetime of frivolous spending. It's you I worry about."

"Well, stop. I'll make it without it."

The fierceness with which he spoke had me closing my mouth.

Adrian paused for a moment as if he was trying to gather his thoughts, and then said, "The company isn't my dream. It never was. And I know it isn't yours either."

I wanted to argue, but I wouldn't lie to him. There were other things I wanted to do with my life, *was* doing with my life, and they had nothing to do with the legacy of Kipos International. A pang of guilt hit me for even having those thoughts. The company was all that we had left of Papa.

"I know what you're thinking, and you need to let it go. Papa wouldn't want us to hold on to something that made us miserable."

"So, what are you saying? I won't let Dara win. She's taken so much from our family."

"I have a plan for us once I have those shares." A wicked smile touched Adrian's lips. "And working for the

Lykaios brothers is a way to achieve it. All I ask is that you trust me."

I stared at my gorgeous brother with his piercing sky-blue eyes, model good looks, and a soul so much older than a twenty-year-old should have. He wouldn't work with Pierce, Zack, and especially Hagen without weighing the consequences or analyzing the situation from every angle. It wouldn't surprise me if he took the skills he learned and created an empire more prominent than what his mentors owned.

Adrian stood and came to sit beside me on the couch, pushing my feet down and then laying his head in my lap as he'd done since he was a toddler. Without thought, I began to play with his hair.

"Will you trust me, Penny? For once let me take on some of the burden."

I loved this boy...*man*...so much. He was so much like Papa.

Tears burned the backs of my eyes.

No matter how much I wanted to, I couldn't shield him in a protective cocoon.

Releasing a sigh, I said, "I trust you. You're the only one I have ever trusted."

"Good." He sat up, reached into his back pocket, and pulled out a card, handing it to me. "I knew you'd see reason. Be there at eleven thirty tomorrow."

I glanced at the card and felt my heart skip a beat. It was the address for Hagen's new restaurant. The one that would open next week and was reported as the most indulgent and opulent of any restaurant-lounge in Vegas.

"Why am I meeting with Hagen?"

"Because he has agreed to help you get the answers to the questions you're too afraid to pursue. While I work my side, you find out the truth about Papa."

CHAPTER TWO

Hagen

"DOES calm ruthlessness come naturally to you or is it a trait you learned on the job?"

"You're one to talk," I said to my younger brother Zacharias, lifting a tumbler of whiskey to my lips and watching the dancers set up for the opening of my new restaurant and nightclub next door. "All three of us are cut from the same cloth, and that would be Collin Dimitri Lykaios."

"Speak for yourself. I have a heart that beats in my chest," Pierce, my other brother, added before he winked at a passing server who'd caught his eye when he'd arrived for what I liked to call the weekly Lykaios brothers roundup.

I snorted. "So says the man who plotted revenge against the woman who dumped him when he was barely old enough to grow pubes."

"Great visual, asshole." Zack picked up his phone, scanned it, responded to the message, and set it back on the table without blinking an eye. "So how are we supposed to handle the fallout?"

Zack, Pierce, and I ran Vegas. It may sound conceited, but it was true. Others may have big projects and casinos, but they all knew that one word from any one of us and all their endeavors would come screeching to a halt.

Case in point, the situation Zack was reaming me about.

"Since he broke it, he has to fix it," Pierce interjected.

Shrugging my shoulders, I released a breath. "You two pussies didn't want to get your hands dirty. I just made it very clear to the foreman that if he messes with the business dealings of one Lykaios brother, he messes with all of us."

"Yeah, but the dipshit turned tail and ran. Now I'm short a construction foreman, out over one hundred grand, and delayed on the hotel build-out." Zack picked up a few nuts sitting in a bowl in the center of the table and popped them in his mouth

"Cry me a river. That's chump change. You make more than that in less than a minute."

The one thing Zacharias Lykaios wasn't short on was money. He gambled and won, both literally and through real estate. There were few risks he wouldn't take.

Zack shrugged. "Money's money."

"I'm not sure why you're bitching to me. It's not like I beat his ass or anything. It was a very civilized conversation."

"Sure, I buy that." Pierce shook his head. "You probably made him piss himself when you walked up."

I looked down at myself. I was probably the most laidback brother out of the three of us. Pierce was the most volatile of all of us. His emotions motivated him in ways that were only going to cause him grief. And then there was Zack. He was most sensitive and most ruthless. His whole world revolved around his end goal—the destruction of our father. But that had nothing to do with me. I'd closed the door on Collin years ago.

It would take more than a chump foreman to piss me off. I'd learned long ago, anger and temper only got me so far. Cold, calm efficiency garnered greater and more effective reactions.

"For the record—" I lifted my tumbler and sipped my drink, "—I never once raised my voice or threatened him with bodily harm. I only made it clear that our legal team would make it very hard for him to procure future contracts with any organization if he didn't get his act in gear. It was all on the up-and-up."

"Cold is what it was. You love playing up that reputation of yours."

"It worked. Didn't it?" I said, lifting a brow.

I could deny my past added to the "don't fuck with me" reputation. But then again, when one is thrown out onto the streets as a teen, one does what they have to. It's either survive and join the underworld or get eaten by it.

Though, I wasn't involved in half of the shit people assumed I was.

"You're such an ass," Zack said. "Next time I'll handle it myself."

"Would you rather I'd punched him as you suggested, pretty boy? My way is cleaner."

"At least with Z's way, they aren't going to assume a mob hit is in their future."

"Sometimes I really wish I'd drowned you both at birth."

"It wouldn't have worked. I do have six gold medals in swimming. And Zack here was the baby and everyone's favorite. So, Mom would have kicked your ass."

"Assholes," I muttered.

"I can't wait to see the woman who melts the ice in your veins." Zack smirked at Pierce and gestured with his thumb at me. "I bet the frozen tundra he calls a temper will erupt at every turn and then maybe he'll feel something like us mere mortals."

"You'll be waiting a lifetime or two. She doesn't exist. Women have a place in my life, and long-term isn't one of them."

With the lifestyle I lived, I'd never had a shortage of companions to stand by my side or keep my bed warm. Nothing ever lasted more than a few weeks.

By my choice, not theirs.

Yeah, it was cold, but there was no point in stringing someone along and giving them false hope. Anyone I was involved with knew from the beginning that what we had was no strings and with a finite expiration date.

"Case in point," Zack said, "this proves you have something other than hot blood that runs in your veins. At least, I can say I've had a bad relationship or two to keep me from anything serious. You act like relationships are a plague."

"Whatever. I like my life the way it is. No complications, no regrets. Simple and easy." I leaned back in my chair and lifted my glass in my brothers' directions before taking a deep gulp.

"I call bullshit." Pierce smirked with a gleam in his eyes.

"Meaning?"

"There's only one woman who has always gotten under your skin."

"And who might that be?"

A look passed between Zack and Pierce that made me want to punch both of them.

In unison, they said, "Persephone Kipos."

Immediately an image of the beautiful goddess with golden skin she'd inherited from her Indian mother and her father's piercing emerald eyes appeared in my mind. She was a man's walking wet dream with curves one could hold on to while driving in deep and lips meant to wrap around a fat cock.

Fuck, what the hell was I doing? Focus, dumbass.

"Good try, but I'm too old for her."

"Keep telling yourself that lie if you want to, but we know the truth. That girl has been giving you a hard-on since she hit puberty."

I'd be damned if I confirmed or denied Pierce's claim. Persephone was someone a man like me could want from a distance. She was beauty, smarts, curves, and innocence. My touch would corrupt her and bring her into a world that could cost her everything. It was better I never acted on the mutual attraction we'd skirted around for the last decade. Distant friendship was where our relationship would remain.

"I'll take your silence as a confirmation. Too bad she

lives in a gilded cage, and her stepmother won't let her anywhere near us." Pierce paused and then continued. "Especially you…"

"That's because our brother here was the one man Dara Kipos couldn't seduce. Hell hath no fury and all that," Zack added.

"That's old news. She's moved on to barely legal pool boys."

"You are the reason her precious son works for us under the radar. Imagine the shitstorm Dara will unleash if she finds out we're grooming Adrian to take her job." Zack picked up his phone again, scanned something on the screen, responded and then set it back on the table. It was more than likely the latest stock updates and trade orders.

The man never stopped working. I wasn't lazy by any means, but I had the ability to turn it off once in a while.

"Speaking of Adrian," Pierce said. "That boy is brilliant. The places he can hack and the information he has the ability to acquire is remarkable."

"Plus, the kid has balls," I added.

Adrian Kipos had somehow circumvented my security to enter one of my most exclusive and restricted parties, walked up to me, and without blinking said, "If you want to prevent your data from being hacked, you need to hire me."

At first, I'd thought the little boy I'd bought ice cream for had lost his mind. Then he'd pulled up his phone and showed me how he'd infiltrated HPZ Holdings, the conglomerate my brothers and I had created for our different ventures. My brothers and I were floored. We had implemented the most high-level cybersecurity money could buy and here was a nineteen-year-old college sophomore cracking our system. Needless to say, we hired him. All Adrian asked for was to learn how to run an international organization like the one he'd inherit when he turned twenty-one and never to let his mother know what he was doing.

For the last year and a half, he'd taken on any job we gave him, and to our amazement, continued to evade our security. Zack jokingly called Adrian our own personal Hermes, after the Greek trickster god who could obtain and send information as well as infiltrate any known place.

"That he does," Zack agreed. "Too bad his mother has no idea he is planning to overthrow her in the very near future."

"We are going to need to make sure nothing happens to him. I have no doubt his mother would prevent him from obtaining control of Kipos International." Pierce frowned.

Zack nodded. "The only saving grace that boy has is Penny. She gave up her life for him. She's more a mother to him than the woman who gave birth to him."

"Adrian is too smart not to know that he has to cover his back. It's Penny I worry about." Pierce watched me, and

I knew he was trying to gauge my reaction. "Dara will destroy her to maintain control of the company."

If there was one thing I knew, it was that Persephone Kipos wasn't the docile flower she allowed the world to see. The girl had secrets, ones I'd discovered recently— ones that would knock the conniving stepmother off her ass.

"I wouldn't discount her cunning. She is so much more than what she lets the world believe." I swirled the aromatic liquor. "Now If you two are done analyzing my sex life and drinking my limited-edition whiskey, I have a lunch meeting to attend."

"With who and about what?" Zack asked.

I couldn't hide the smile that touched my lips. They were probably going to shit themselves when I told them. "It's a business proposition with someone I like to call Starlight."

Penny

"I NEED ALL the latest analyses of the recent batches," I said to my assistant and cousin, Anaya, as I walked around the distillation vats. "I also need to know any updates on the property negotiations for the European manufacturing locations."

"You'll have it by the end of the day." Anaya paused. "By the way, we received another offer from Lykaios Holdings for a face-to-face meeting. They sent over an extremely lucrative proposal for the exclusive use of Firewater for their hotels, casinos, and venues."

I sighed and shook my head. "The answer is as it always is, Ana. No. Collin isn't someone I plan to now or ever work with."

"Won't you consider meeting with him, if only to see what he has to say?"

"Wait a second." I studied Anaya. "Does Collin know about my involvement with Firewater?"

"No. I swear. No one outside our circle knows anything about who owns PSK Distilleries. According to Henna, he loves our whiskey and would love to have distribution rights to the product."

"Even if I considered his offer, I couldn't accept it. I have a deal established with Hagen, Pierce, and Zack. I won't renege on our contract."

"Would you entertain a limited distribution deal? Collin and Henna have been working their asses off to reestablish Lykaios Holdings's appeal. He isn't the same man he was a decade ago. He's done more for Henna and me than anyone could ever imagine. He has a lot of regrets, and most of them revolve around his sons."

My cousins Henna and Anaya Anthony were the daughters of my mom's sister Lena, whom I called Lena Masi, and my deceased uncle Victor Anthony. They had an adoration for Collin Lykaios that I could never understand.

No, that wasn't true. I could understand it, even if I couldn't comprehend why Collin had changed his ways.

About fifteen years earlier, Uncle Victor had been indicted on charges of embezzlement and tax evasion. He'd swindled nearly a billion dollars from his business partners, friends, and family. Among them was Collin Lykaios. Collin had lost almost fifty million dollars in investments. It had been a national scandal, and even more so after Uncle Victor had committed suicide to avoid prosecution.

In order to escape the fallout and backlash of all the angry investors, Lena Masi had left the state and assumed a completely different identity. What was most surprising in all of this was that Collin had been instrumental in keeping my aunt and cousins safe. He'd gone as far as having new birth records, bank accounts, and school histories established. Then when they were older, he'd funded their college educations and offered them jobs in his organization. Henna had accepted and now ran

Lykaios Holdings, but Anaya was a science and computer nerd who, like me, enjoyed behind-the-scenes tinkering.

I could accept my cousins' loyalty to Collin, especially after all he'd done for them. However, I had my own loyalties, and it was to the three young boys Collin had disowned when they were barely grown. I wasn't sure I would ever be able to get over the fact Hagen had lived on the streets for a time because he'd had nowhere to go. I know to this day the man's dark reputation was something he'd had to build to avoid becoming a Vegas statistic.

I could still remember Papa's anger at Collin when he'd heard about what he'd done to Hagen. Papa had driven around the streets of Vegas looking for a skinny teen with looks too attractive to survive without coming out unscathed.

Shaking the thoughts from my head, I looked at Anaya. "I love you, but you have to stop beating this dead horse. Praising Collin's acts of service won't change the fact he hurt three people I care about."

"I know." She released a resigned breath. "It's hard for me to reconcile the man he is now with the one he was before. Just so you know, he worries about you too. He's seen how Dara treats you."

Sadness hit my heart. Collin had been one of my favorite people when I was younger. He'd told the most amazing stories and always encouraged me to pursue science when "good Greek and Indian girls" were supposed to focus on family and culture over their studies. If I was honest with myself, it was the seed Collin had planted that had given me the push to research the process of aged whiskey. And because of what I learned, I was able to create Firewater, a whiskey that tasted like one aged for twenty years but without waiting for the results. Science and technology had the ability to defy time.

"You of all people should know, the mousy pushover the world sees isn't who I am... Never mind. I can't think about that right now, or Collin. The goal is to analyze the next batch and set Adrian up to succeed when he takes over and Dara is history."

CHAPTER THREE

Penny

A LITTLE AFTER eleven thirty I arrived at Ida Astro for my lunch with Hagen. I took a deep breath and waited for the valet to open my door.

"Wow, this is some car." The awe in the attendant's face made me smile.

I may have the world believing I was a weakling, but there was one thing I was known for. And it was my love for sports cars, especially refurbished classic ones. I'd inherited my obsession for fast vehicles from my parents, who'd met at a racetrack in Greece when Mama had illegally entered my grandfather's Aston Martin and won. She'd been barely sixteen and had snuck out of her gilded cage overlooking the Mediterranean. The fact she'd won the race hadn't mattered to my grandfather. He'd seen it as being corrupted by European morals and had sent her to live in India for two years with a distant uncle. However, when she'd returned, Papa had all but kidnapped her away from my grandfather, and within a month they'd been married.

I drove the very car now, a 1965 Aston Martin DB5. Every time I was behind the wheel, I felt close to my two amazing parents.

"Thank you," I said as I slipped out of the car, adjusted my skirt, and set my handbag on my arm.

"I'll park it next to Mr. Lykaios's Spider."

I glanced to the '66 Alfa Romeo in a nearly empty parking lot.

Of course, Hagen would have the same vice I had. The man was all things dangerous, and therefore I was attracted to him.

The thought of him had anxiety seeping into my stomach. Shit. I'd hoped the drive would calm my nerves.

I had barely interacted with him for the last fifteen years, and here I was about to ask him to help me find out the truth of Papa's death.

After Adrian had sprung the news of the meeting he'd set up, I'd grilled him on all the details of what he'd told Hagen. Adrian insisted that all he said was that I needed help with a personal matter. My brother was a man of few words, so I assumed that was the extent of the details he'd given. The fact Hagen had agreed without question added to the uncertainty I was feeling.

I closed my eyes for a moment, gathering my courage. I could do this. I could meet with the man who'd starred in a majority of my fantasies and ask him to help me find out if Dara had orchestrated Papa's death.

I expected there to be a price for his help. Hagen had a reputation of expecting payment in kind for his assistance in any matter. The problem was that I'd probably agree to anything he asked if it meant Dara was out of our lives for good.

Maybe I'd be able to convince Hagen to give me something else in addition to his help. Something I'd never have considered before, but hell, I was already stepping into his world. Or maybe I'd just offer it without reciprocation. I couldn't think of any better way to lose my V card than with a bad boy like Hagen.

My pulse jumped just thinking about the possibility.

Snap out of it, Penny. You are about to have lunch with the man known as the Master of Sin. Your libido needs to take a back burner to logic.

"Ms. Kipos?" A woman approached me, who I could only assume was the hostess. She had long blond hair and legs for miles. The color of her lips matched the form-fitting dress she wore. She was breathtaking and what I would dub very Vegas.

I smiled at her, and she responded with a genuine one of her own. "Yes, that's me."

"My name is Camille." She shook my hand. "I'm the manager of Ida Astro. If you would follow me. Mr. Lykaios is waiting for you on the veranda."

Okay, here it goes. I squared my shoulders and followed Camille inside.

The interior of the restaurant was bright with clean lines and glass sculptures everywhere. This was nothing like the dark and indulgent atmosphere Hagen's other establishments were known for. There was a polished elegance to the place. In fact, the color scheme was very similar to what I'd have chosen, if I had a home outside of the corporate one I used.

It wasn't as if I didn't have the funds to buy a house. I'd gone so far as to put an offer on a dream home in Summerlin, Nevada, a small suburb of Vegas that would have allowed me to step away from all that Sin City was known for. But almost immediately I'd decided against it. It was better to let Dara think she had ultimate control of my life. Until Adrian took over the company, I would let Dara think my inheritance from my mom was tied up until I was thirty as she believed and be the dutiful but inconsequential stepdaughter she tolerated.

As we walked farther into the room, I noticed there were chandeliers of various shades strategically positioned throughout the giant space, giving the area an elegant atmosphere without looking overly crowded.

A bartender looked up as we neared and smiled. He was opening a case of Firewater, one of a very exclusive bottling that I only allowed to be distributed in limited supply and only to the right clientele.

It still shocked me how much of a demand there was for my elderflower-infused whiskey. I'd introduced my whiskey a little under eight years ago to the market and had garnered a loyal following. It wasn't until three years ago when an Oscar-winning movie star had thrown a party with the whiskey as the main ingredient in everything he served that Firewater's demand had grown to an astronomical level. Literally hours after the party had ended, every A-lister, high-end hotel, and entertainment venue wanted the whiskey.

I grinned to myself. Amazing how the right type of marketing can launch a product.

"Would you like a taste?" Camille said, catching my gaze.

"I'm fine, thank you."

"It's a special reserve. Mr. Lykaios had to sweet-talk the distributor to get six bottles. We were lucky enough to get a sip today. It is quite indulgent."

I shook my head. "I'm good."

Camille gave me a shocked look that I turned down the alcohol then continued through the restaurant.

As we walked through the doors leading to the veranda, my breath hitched. Hagen leaned a hand against the railing that overlooked the strip and talked on the phone. This man personified the sexy-as-sin Greek god name the tabloids had given him. The tailored suit he wore fit his toned body to perfection. His face was all hard lines and angles with a symmetry that usually was only achievable through the expert precision of a surgeon. The only things giving away his bad-boy vibe were the tattoos on his hand and the ones I glimpsed drawn along the skin of the open collar of his shirt.

Immediately a low throb began to pulse between my legs. He hadn't even looked in my direction, and I had a deep need to jump him.

At that moment, Hagen lifted his gaze to mine, and a wicked glint entered his eyes.

Why did he always stare at me like that? And why did my body react to that look?

This was the reason I avoided him at all costs. No one could know how he affected me, especially not Dara, or she'd find some way to hold it over my head.

Hagen ended his call and walked in my direction. When he was a foot away, he grasped my hand and lifted it to his lips. A shiver shot through me the second his lips grazed my skin. Then he kissed my cheek, and his intoxicating scent of spiced cologne and soap engulfed my senses.

"Persephone Starlight Kipos. It is good to see you. You look beautiful as always."

Why did his use of my full name make a tingle shoot through my core? I had two of the stupidest names on the planet. No Greek girl should ever be named Persephone and Starlight. I still have no idea what my parents were smoking when they decided on that one.

After a few moments of staring at him, my brain fired, and I said, "It's nice to see you too."

Something about him had me all tongue-tied in a way Pierce and Zack never made me feel. And the thought of dreaming about touching them, wanting to do deliciously dirty things to them made me want to gag, not squeeze my thighs together.

I was going to need a long, cold shower and a session with my vibrator when I got home.

Hagen released my hand and gestured to a table set up with fine china and an array of appetizers.

"I wasn't sure what you liked so I had the chef make a variety of things."

"I'm sure all of it will be perfect. Chef Gustav hasn't made a dish I haven't liked."

"How could I forget? You used to say you were that annoying bitch that made the stuff the chefs cooked on TV."

Heat crept up my cheeks as I slid into my seat.

I'd said that at a party Dara had thrown where the food tasted like dirt spread on toast. I'd been all of sixteen to Hagen's twenty-three. I'd spent the night hungry and irritable. Around midnight, when I'd finally called it a night and made my way to my bedroom, I'd found a takeout bag from one of my favorite restaurants in Vegas. I'd known Hagen was responsible, but I'd never figured out how he managed to sneak it into my bedroom with all the security Dara had positioned around the family house.

"A gentleman isn't supposed to remind a lady of when she's made unladylike comments."

Hagen took his seat and lifted a brow. "I've never pretended to be a gentleman, Starlight. Besides, I'm almost positive you thoroughly enjoyed the Kobe beef burger I had waiting for you in your room that night."

My mouth watered thinking of the juicy burger. "If you want to know the truth, I inhaled it within minutes. I'd spent most of the week before the party starving since Dara had decided to put me on a diet for the party and hoped I'd lose a few pounds."

A frown marred his face, but before he could say

anything, I spoke. "Want to tell me how you got past all the security to sneak me a burger?"

His eyes crinkled at the corners. "Some secrets are better left unsaid. Who knows, I may need to rescue the princess in the tower next time, instead of commandeering a meal for her."

If he only knew how right his words were.

A server came to the table and set up a serving of Firewater whiskey.

"You do realize that is almost a thousand dollars an ounce?" I stared at the reddish-gold-tinged liquid that was set in front of both Hagen and me.

"I'm sure I can make a bargain with the manufacturer for a few more bottles." He picked up the tumbler and swallowed the drink in one gulp.

I licked my lips and felt a sense of panic replace the arousal I had felt moments earlier. He couldn't know. No one in my world knew. Well, maybe a few people, and they were loyal to the bone.

The look in his eyes told me he was more aware of things than I hoped.

"I guess that all depends on what you offer."

"It isn't so much what I want to give but what is requested of me."

"Hagen, what are you playing at?" I said, trying to keep a tone of calmness in my voice.

"This isn't a game, Starlight." He said my name in a way that sounded a bit possessive. "You're here for something that could put you in danger."

"How would you know what I'm here for?" I knew Adrian would never lie.

"Your brother is a brilliant boy, but the only reason he would give you over to the devil was if a bargain with him would garner the answers to who killed your father."

"Are you saying you're the devil?"

He held my gaze, and the desire reignited. And if I wasn't mistaken, something flared in his sapphire eyes. "I've been called worse. So, tell me. Are you here to make a deal with a man who could ruin your pristine reputation?"

What if I want it ruined?

"What is it going to cost me?"

He stroked his stubbly jaw with a hand covered in tattoos. "Let me see. I may want all of the next shipment of Firewater."

I opened my mouth to deny I had any pull but he spoke again.

"Or the exclusive rights to the elderflower you have been secretly developing for your distilleries... Or..."

I clenched my fingers on the edge of the table. I knew better than to think he would want something simple. "Or?" I probed.

He covered my hand with his. "Or you in my bed. To

do with whatever I want, whenever I want, however I want."

Dear God. He hadn't just said that. I pressed my thighs together, trying to relieve the dirty visions popping into my mind.

"Did I shock you, Starlight?"

My temper flared through the haze of desire. He was fucking with me. We'll see about that.

Okay, Penny, you aren't a pushover. Time to stop the pretense.

I leaned toward him until we were nearly face-to-face and said, "What if I said you don't need a bargain to have me in your bed? That I would let you do whatever you wanted to me, whenever, and however?"

Shock and surprise crossed his face, and he sat back, releasing my hand. Then a deep laugh rumbled from him, making some of the staff around us stop and turn in our direction.

"There she is. The girl who was hiding under the prim-and-proper conservative facade."

Just as I was about to respond, a man approached us. He was dressed in a leather jacket, and there was no hiding the side piece he had strapped to his body.

"Mr. Lykaios, we have a situation that requires your attention."

Hagen released an irritated sigh. "If you'll excuse me a moment."

I nodded.

Hagen rose and followed the man who I could only assume worked for him. I watched Hagen move to a section of the restaurant where a group of men stood. Some words were said, and the next thing I knew, Hagen dodged a punch and landed one of his own, sending the man who had swung to the floor.

My heartbeat drummed into my ears.

What the fuck was happening? The man who attacked Hagen was twice his size and now was on the ground pinned by three of Hagen's security.

They cuffed his arms behind his back, and then hauled the man up. As he got to his feet, he looked through the window at me. Something about him was familiar, but I couldn't place him. Hagen followed the direction he looked, and a scowl appeared on his face.

He stepped in front of the man, blocking his view of me. After a few more words, Hagen came back outside.

His face was a bit flushed and a line creased between his brows. "Sorry about that. Mike used to work for an associate of mine, and he wasn't ready to accept he'd lost his job. Unfortunately for me, I had to be the messenger."

In my personal opinion, there was nothing to be sorry about. I was the lucky gal who was privileged to see Vegas's bad boy in action. The fact I was super turned on by it told me I definitely wanted in his pants.

I kept my inappropriate thoughts to myself.

Hagen set his hand on the back of my chair. "I hate to cut our lunch short, but I have to handle the Mike situation."

I felt a twinge of disappointment, but covered it quickly and said, "It's okay. I have to take care of a few things before I head back to the office anyway."

"I want a raincheck. And next time, I promise we won't be disturbed."

The idea of being alone with Hagen again sent a wave of desire to my core. I should say no but there was no way I could resist another lunch with Hagen.

"I'll hold you to it." I smiled up and for a split second, there was a gleam in his blue eyes that made it seem as if he'd read my thoughts.

He offered me his hand, and I slid mine across his palm. The contact felt like electricity shot through me, and from the desire in Hagen's eyes, I'd say he experienced the same thing.

I stood and nearly moaned when his palm grazed my waist. He led me through the restaurant and in the direction of the exit. My stomach churned, and I realized I had no desire to leave, even with the potential of another lunch. I wanted to explore the promise I'd seen in Hagen's gaze.

Just as we crossed the threshold, he asked, "Would you like to see the interior of the new club?"

Nyx, named after the Greek god of the night, was supposed to be the jewel of all of Hagen's clubs, and I wasn't going to pass up an opportunity to see inside.

"Yes," I said a bit too breathlessly, then added. "Don't you have to attend to the Mike situation?"

"He can wait. Your time is more important."

It was as if he knew I wanted to stay a little longer.

We took a set of stairs that led to the underground of Ida, the resort that Hagen ran with his brothers.

"It is easiest to enter the club through the tunnels."

I nodded and followed him through the maze until we entered a hallway that opened into the main dance room of the club. It had the same atmosphere as the restaurant but with the extra decadent vibe. There were splashes of a reddish gold throughout, in the accent pieces and small details of the walls. From the ceiling hung cages that looked like tasteful chandeliers but I knew would hold dancers in various states of dress.

Hagen saw where I was staring. "There's nothing wrong with giving the illusion of classy while indulging in the darker and naughtier side of life."

"Makes sense. This place is beautiful. Different from

your others."

"I designed it around the spirit that makes up all the signature drinks we'll serve."

I turned to him. "Is that right? I hope you're ready to spend a pretty penny."

"Starlight, the penny is more than worth it."

His words made a knot form in my gut. There was no denying he knew who was behind the coveted whiskey. But what troubled me was why he and his brothers would design a hotel, casino, club, and restaurant around it.

"Come this way. They're still installing the final lighting, and I don't want us to get in the way."

He walked over to a wall, scanned his eye. A door popped out, and he led me inside.

"Let me guess. One of Adrian's inventions."

A smile touched Hagen's lips that gave me visions of what he could do with that mouth.

"Your brother takes his craft seriously."

The door locked behind us, and almost immediately I felt the atmosphere of the office we'd entered change. There was an undercurrent of arousal and need flowing, and it definitely wasn't one-sided.

I leaned my back against the door and studied the predator in the impeccable suit before me. What was it about him that made me want to throw caution out the window?

"So, what now?" I asked as he took my clutch from my hand and threw it on a nearby table.

"You tell me."

I pressed my palm to his chest, loving the heat that radiated through the material of his shirt.

"Tell me you feel this."

"Yes."

"My excuse is the adrenaline from the asshole earlier. What's yours?"

I licked my lips and watched his eyes dilate. "Do I need one?"

He stepped forward. "No, you don't." His mouth covered mine.

Dear God, he tasted amazing, whiskey and his own natural essence. His lips were soft, softer than I ever expected. His tongue found its way against mine, and the kiss grew deeper. He rolled and glided, making my mind cloud with a need suppressed for too long.

I found my head jerked back in a tight grip as our mouths continued to duel. We ate at each other as if we were starved.

My arms pulled him closer, wanting nothing more than to feel all of him against me. His hard length pressed into my stomach and my core flooded with desire.

I knew it would be like this if I ever got a chance to kiss him. He was all-consuming and demanding, everything I could ever want. Logic should tell me to stop, to take a step back and think about what going any further would mean. But all I could do was drown in the cascade of desire.

Hagen released my hair, and his hands slid up my thighs, pulling them apart and wrapping them around his waist. He rubbed his rock-hard cock along the seam of my pussy and against my aching clit.

"Hagen," I moaned, wanting more. "I need."

"I know what you need. I'm just not sure you can handle it." He licked down my throat and then nipped the juncture of my neck and shoulder.

I jerked, and my core clenched, arching into the pleasure-pain.

"More. Please. More." I couldn't believe I was begging. Now if only I knew what I begged for.

Hagen began to grind his cock back and forth against the sensitive nerves at the apex of my cleft, creating a rhythm that had every cell in my body screaming.

"Come for me, Starlight." His hand slid farther up my skirt and then his thumb began to stroke my clit.

I detonated, throwing my head back as stars flashed behind my eyes. My pussy spasmed and contracted. I lost all sense of place and time.

My arousal flooded through my core, soaking his thumb and bringing out a groan from his exploring mouth.

"I can't wait to taste your sweet cunt. One day you will come while I fuck you with my mouth."

His words spurred another contraction.

Holy fuck. Dirty talk got me off.

Slowly, I came down from the best orgasm of my life and realized I was now sitting on Hagen's lap. His erection was a brand under my bottom, and his breath was ragged. I looked into his blue depths that almost seemed black since his pupils ate up his eyes.

I tried to reach for his pants, but he stilled my movement.

"I won't take you. No matter how much I want to. Watching you come apart has to be enough."

He threw his head back against the couch and closed his eyes, releasing a pained breath.

"I don't understand. You know as well as I do that there's more to this attraction than we wanted to admit. It's been there for as long as I can remember."

He lifted his head. "Starlight, if I take you, the world you know will change. You won't be the innocent and naive Kipos heiress anymore. My reputation will taint yours. Being with me could mean Dara pushing you out of your father's company, and I don't think you're ready for that."

The mention of Dara was like throwing a bucket of ice water on my desire.

I slid from Hagen's lap and immediately missed the heat of him. I rested my face in my palms.

"It wouldn't matter if we slept together or not. Dara would take everything from Adrian the second she got the opportunity. If I don't stop her, she may orchestrate something like what happened to Papa to get rid of Adrian."

I was going to stop her, and it all revolved around Papa's death. "Whatever the cost, I want you to use your connections to find out the truth about Papa."

"Then you know my terms."

I turned to him. "There were three options. Which one?"

"So you're admitting Firewater, and the patent for elderflower used in it, belongs to you?"

"I am doing no such thing."

"So you're willing to sleep with me despite the fact you could lose your job and your ability to keep an eye on your father's company?"

I opened my mouth to answer, but he cut me off, cupping my face and placing a thumb on my lips.

"No. Think about it first. What I want won't be on your terms, but mine. It isn't sweet and gentle. It will require you to give yourself to me completely. I will corrupt you, and you won't want it to stop. In the end, I will ruin you."

CHAPTER FOUR

Hagen

I ENTERED my penthouse on the thirty-sixth floor of Ida. Zack, Pierce, and I each lived in separate penthouses at one of the major HPZ casino-hotels. It was our way to maintain a presence and keep anyone from getting the idea that the brothers weren't a unit. Yes, Zack was the brains behind the properties, but none of them would work without the investment of each brother.

I threw my suit jacket on a nearby couch and walked toward the stocked bar. I picked up a bottle of Macallen 25 and poured myself three fingers of the classic scotch. As I set the decanter down, my gaze moved to the reserve bottle of Firewater, making me shake my head.

That woman was as stubborn as they came. Starlight would rather agree to sleep with me than reveal she'd created one of the most sought-after whiskeys in the world. Under the mouse facade was a brilliant chemist who'd analyzed the properties of the historically best-rated spirits and created her uniquely smooth concoction in a lab, of all things.

It was only sheer luck that I discovered where Firewater was created and then subsequently the mastermind behind the whiskey. One of my researchers for my restaurants was on holiday in India, and a local mentioned an elderflower spirit distillery. He'd investigated the area and then recognized Persephone as she sat at a bar near the building. After I learned this, I did a little digging and discovered she, no, her company, PSK, held the patent on four strands of elderflower plants. It immediately became apparent she was behind the high-dollar whiskey that had taken the world by storm.

I knew if I'd found out the identity of the reclusive owner of the distillery, then others eventually would too. Persephone was a genius in her own right, but stealthy she was not. There had even been times I thought someone would kidnap her or kill her when she'd venture into areas of the world that had unique elderflower plants but were considered dangerous even by the locals. She seemed to thrive on research and negotiating her most significant ingredient for her experiments without a care for her safety.

She was too damn trusting.

The number of times she'd given me a near heart attack with her adventures were too numerous to count. So I'd spent the last two years discreetly making sure she stayed protected and used my contacts to snub out any rumors around the owner of PSK.

The fact I'd created businesses around Firewater may speak to my obsession with Starlight, but then again until today I never imagined touching her, let alone making her orgasm, outside of my dreams.

God, I could still hear her cries of release and pleasure. I'd never seen anything like it. She was a siren with an aura of innocence wrapped in a body meant for sin.

Why had I waited so long? She'd wanted me as long as I'd craved her. For over a decade, I'd seen it on her face every time we were in a room together.

Who was I kidding? Collin Lykaios's words were drilled into my head, and for some damn reason, I believed him.

"Do you think I haven't seen how you look at her? That girl is too good for the likes of you. You're trash compared to her. If you lay one filthy hand on her body, I will ruin you, boy. You're better off warming Dara's bed. She's partial to lowlife scum."

Rage filled my body as Collin's words echoed in my mind. He'd known I'd felt that way about myself and had preyed on it.

Just another way he'd tried to control me.

The fact I'd gotten involved in the underworld of Las Vegas wasn't something I was proud of, but the blame could be set at my father's feet.

What kind of man threw his seventeen-year-old son out of his house for getting drunk one time with friends?

Collin Lykaios, that's who.

He'd given me less than twenty minutes to pack my shit and leave while ignoring the pleas from my weeping mother and the terrified looks of my younger brothers.

Collin had gone as far as threatening anyone who offered me shelter with omens of ruining their financial livelihoods. I'd spent the next three months moving from shelter to shelter. That was until a gang of stray kids had beat the shit out of me for being too pretty and then tried to rape me. I'd fought my way out of their hold and took off. After that day, I never returned to any shelter.

If Draco Jackson hadn't found me scared out of my mind and walking the strip with all my worldly possessions in a backpack and starving, I'd probably have died on the streets. He'd heard about what Collin had done and ordered his network of spies to look for me.

The mobster had cleaned me up, given me a place to stay, and a job.

What I'd had to do at the beginning of my life working for Jackson was the reason I had my current reputation. But I would forever owe the man who saved my life. As surrogate fathers go, Jackson wasn't ideal but better than the one who'd supplied my DNA.

I threw back the tumbler of scotch I held in my hand and swallowed the amber liquid in one gulp, letting it burn down my throat and dull my senses.

Walking out toward the three-hundred-sixty-degree windows, I stared across the Strip to the Lykaios Towers. It was the pinnacle hotel and casino in Collin's empire. The last time I'd stepped foot in that place was the day my mother had died. She wanted to say goodbye, and for some reason, Collin had approved the visit.

I guessed Papa Dearest wanted to have a clean conscience when his wife took her last breaths after battling breast cancer for nearly a year.

Now here I was a decade and a half later, living a life beyond what I could ever have imagined. For the most part, I'd left the grime of the Vegas underworld behind. The only thing missing was... I wouldn't go there.

I didn't need Collin's word to tell me that she was out of my league. She deserved someone who wasn't tainted. Someone who wouldn't expect things of her beyond her safe world. Someone who didn't have his hands dirtied by a past filled with drugs, murder, and prostitution.

Tomorrow I'd call her and tell her I'd help her without anything in return. It would kill me, but I'd do it.

She was the only decent thing I'd ever experienced in my life.

God, I could still taste her on my lips. Could still feel her nipples pebble through her shirt. Could still hear the low moan of desire she mewled when our tongues tangled and passion had overwhelmed her. It had taken all my willpower not to lay her across my desk and bury myself balls-deep inside her slick, wet cunt.

Fucking hell.

Now I was going to spend the evening with a raging case of blue balls.

The elevator dinged, making me groan. I quickly pulled out my tucked shirt to cover my hard-on and turned to see who stepped off.

"You look like a man who needs to either get laid or punch the shit out of someone," Zack said as he entered my penthouse, throwing his suit jacket on top of mine before walking over to my bar. He poured himself a large helping of the Firewater reserve and smiled.

Just as he was about to take a sip, he paused, glanced in my direction, and said, "I say both."

I ignored his remark and asked, "You do realize that

glass of whiskey you're about to drink would cost you nearly four thousand dollars anywhere else?"

Zack shrugged. "And your point is?"

"You're an asshole. Not all of us make the kind of money you make in an hour."

"If you didn't want people drinking it then you shouldn't have it stocked in your bar." He tilted the tumbler against his lips and closed his eyes, savoring the infused whiskey. "Would this piss-poor mood have anything to do with the green-eyed siren you had lunch with today?"

"We never got to lunch." I continued to gaze out at the lights of Las Vegas. "I was interrupted by Mike Popov."

"I can't believe that dick's still coming around. He should be happy you convinced Draco not to take care of him in the way you would have done back in the day."

When I'd first started off working for Draco, I'd posed as his muscle. Even at seventeen, I was a large man. Plus, years of martial arts had kept me lean and muscular. Whenever Draco had a problem, I was sent in to make sure his views were expressed in the correct manner. Usually with a fist and occasionally with a revolver pressed to the temple to make my point.

Outside of a few incidental jobs done as favors for Draco, the days of working as his heavy man were long gone. There was one benefit to the reputation I'd gained working for him—rarely, if ever, did anyone fuck with me or my brothers. No one truly believed I was out of the business and so I let the misconception stand.

"Maybe you should have let Draco's men take care of the matter instead of trying to make nice because you wanted to help out an ex. Kim would have been far better off without her lowlife father."

"That isn't here nor there. Kim asked for a favor, and I delivered. The girl is married and has three kids now. She doesn't need the stress associated with Mike's antics."

"You're the only man I know who remains friends with all of the women who've shared his bed." Zack shook his head.

"At least with my way I don't have to worry about someone putting a hit out on me for being an asshole."

Zack shrugged his shoulders. "Everyone knows where they stand in the end, and there aren't any hopes of reconciliations."

"I can't wait until the day you get a taste of your own medicine."

"Never going to happen. Now tell me what Mike's issue was today."

"Apparently he wasn't happy with the deal you and Draco negotiated and decided to make a scene in front of Starlight. Now I'm going to have to take care of it Draco's way."

Why had I ever agreed to handle the gambler for Draco?

Because you're a sucker for innocent women who need help.

Shit. I'd fucked this up royally. There was no way I could let any of Draco's men clean up my mess.

"Need us to back you up? I have a few guys who owe me a favor or two," Zack said.

"No. It's better neither of you are involved." I ran a hand through my hair. "There is no way of leaving the life, is there?"

"Maybe you can offer him a way out again." Zack watched me, knowing I really didn't want to ship the bastard.

"There's no use. Draco only gives one out. Mike got his chance and blew it. It'll be done by morning."

This was the reason I should never have acted on the attraction to Starlight. She was pure and didn't need to be tainted by me. No matter how much I cleaned my act up, there were aspects of my life that would always pull me back in. If I was lucky, Mike would have skipped town by now, knowing what was coming for him. But with my luck, it was wishful thinking.

"I'm glad he didn't make a bigger scene in front of Starlight and all he got was a punch to the gut."

"Why do you call Penny by the stupid name Starlight? It makes her sound like a stripper."

I whirled around and glared. "Never disrespect her like that again. I don't care if you're my brother, I will rearrange your pretty-boy face."

"Woo. Man, calm the fuck down." Zack raised his hands in surrender. "You know I don't mean anything like that. Hell, she's like my sister. Seriously, you need to get laid."

"Fuck off. And for the record, Starlight is her middle name."

"Well, shit. I forgot about that. Never in a million years would I have believed Kipos would give his daughter a hippy name."

"I doubt he had very much say in it. If you recall, when Ms. Karina wanted something, she got it."

I remembered how much I'd wished Collin had loved Mama in the way Jacob had loved Karina. It was as if the sun, moon, and stars hung by Karina's happiness.

Collin, on the other hand, stayed in a perpetual state of irritation when it came to Mama. He hadn't even batted an eye when Mama had decided to do a world tour with her friends that lasted nearly five months. Even as a thirteen-year-old, I recognized Collin wasn't the type of husband or father other kids had in their lives.

Then again, if Collin hadn't been the insufferable bastard he was, life would have taken a different turn.

Though there was a high probability that I'd have become one of those rich snot-nosed shits I wanted to pummel whenever they acted as the world owed them something for existing. Instead, I'd become the bogeyman who cleaned up their messes and kept them in line.

Fuck, snap out of it, dickhead.

"So I take it Penny wasn't too impressed with the darker side of your life?"

"She didn't seem fazed by it."

If I wasn't mistaken, the flare in her eyes was of pure lust. My thug side had aroused her.

"Then what's the problem?"

"She wants me to help her find out who killed her father. She thinks Dara had something to do with it."

"Well, shit. This could get very dangerous for her, especially if she snoops in areas she shouldn't. I wouldn't put it past Dara to retaliate. I hope you put that tail on Penny as I suggested."

If he only knew how long I'd been watching Starlight's back. He'd probably think I needed to be committed. Yes, I knew that made me sound like a creepy stalker, but I wanted her safe. Especially after I found out she was involved in a very competitive and cutthroat liquor market.

"It's been done. I've had someone on her for a while."

Zack lifted a brow and shook his head. "I say seduce her and get it out of your system."

"You know that's a bad idea. The last thing she needs is a relationship with me that could give Dara the ammunition to oust her from Kipos."

"If it isn't you, she'll find some other way."

"I won't be the cause of her losing her job."

"It may be too late." Zack set his drink on the glass coffee table and began to roll up the sleeves of his button-down shirt.

"Care to fill me in?"

At that moment, the elevator opened again. Pierce walked in, carrying a file box.

Pierce looked at Zack and asked, "Have you brought him up to date?"

"We were getting to it. Since you're here and know the details, why don't you relay the information."

Pierce set the box on the floor, opened the lid, and pulled out a set of folders, handing one to me and then to Zack.

He took a seat in the armchair across me. "I'm about to give you the keys to ensure Persephone Kipos is free from Dara Kipos for good. And if you're a lucky boy, your Starlight will be very grateful."

CHAPTER FIVE

Penny

AROUND SEVEN THIRTY the next morning, I entered the Las Vegas offices of Kipos International. I yawned and took a deep gulp of my home-brewed coffee. I was exhausted, and it wasn't anyone's fault but mine. I'd spent a restless night thinking about Hagen and all that had transpired between us. Mainly focusing on how he'd woken something in my body that I never wanted to go to sleep again.

The last thing I expected when I went to meet Hagen was to end up pinned to a wall and orgasming. Now I wasn't going to lie and say I'd never been fascinated about the idea of Hagen doing delicious dirty things to me.

However, I never thought it would happen in a million years.

My biggest problem was that one taste of Hagen had me craving more, which only meant I was up shit creek.

I couldn't risk Dara's spies following me, especially after finding another surveillance bug in my kitchen. Thank God Adrian had given me a scanner to check for devices.

I'd lucked out yesterday. But it was too risky even to consider meeting with him again, no matter how much my hormones were screaming to do the opposite.

Who was I kidding? The chemistry was too intense for me not to seek Hagen out again.

Maybe a little chat with Adrian was in order. He could give me pointers on how he'd worked for the brothers for years without anyone knowing. I'd learn something from my sneaky baby brother.

Pulling out my access card, I scanned it against the security entrance. The light beeped red, denying me entry.

What the hell?

I scanned the card again, with the same response.

As I tried for the third time, Jeffery, one of the security leads for Kipos, approached me. He'd been with the company for over twenty years, and I knew his loyalty was to Adrian and me, not Dara. He'd told me once that the only reason he hadn't retired by now was that he wanted me to have an ally in Kipos. He was my eyes and ears for things coming down the pipeline of the company.

"Ms. Kipos, follow me. Mrs. Kipos requested your presence." He glanced toward the security cameras, giving me a clue we were being watched.

I nodded and said, "What's going on, Jeff?"

He shrugged. "I couldn't say." Once we cleared the main entrance, he continued, "Mrs. Kipos's personal staff has been here for the past two hours. The only thing I know is that I was to inform them the moment you arrived."

My stomach turned. Could she know about my meeting with Hagen? Of course she could. If my condo was bugged, why wouldn't she put trackers on all my cars...again.

I knew better than to forget to check my car before I headed out yesterday to meet Hagen.

I'd spent all these years jumping through hoops to hide my work for PSK and I overlooked this basic bit of precaution. My security team was going to kick my ass when they found out.

I couldn't think about them right now. My priority was dealing with Dara.

"I know you just checked, but will you have my cars rescanned for trackers?"

"I'll order one as soon as I leave you with Mrs. Kipos."

We walked through a side door and to a bank of elevators. A minute later we arrived on the twenty-sixth floor. The second the doors opened, the three men I liked to call Dara's over-muscled Three Stooges waited for us. They were well over six feet and built like tanks. Rarely, if ever, did they leave her side. I was almost positive they shared her bed on occasion too.

"Ms. Kipos, we require your laptop and company mobile."

I jerked back as Shane, one of the Stooges, tried to grab my shoulder bag. "Do not touch me. I want to know what is going on."

No one said anything.

I stalked toward Dara's office and found Adrian standing there with her.

"As punctual as ever." Dara approached me. "Did you enjoy your liaison with Hagen Lykaios yesterday?"

I glanced at Adrian, who shook his head, giving me the signal that things were pretty bad.

"I have no idea what you are talking about."

"Oh, come off it, Penny. I've known about your little crush on him since you were a snot-nosed teen. I never thought you'd sell yourself to him."

I furrowed my brow and searched the room, trying to make sense of what the hell was going on.

Then my eyes settled on the burly man sitting in the

corner. He seemed engrossed in a newspaper, but I knew his attention was on me. I knew I'd seen him over the years, but I couldn't place him. Probably someone who filled a spot in Dara's bed when she was between nineteen-year-old pool boys and bored with her personal security.

"Who's that?"

"None of your concern. We're here to discuss you."

"Dara, I don't have time for this. I have a meeting with one of our distributors for the Holland project in twenty minutes."

I turned to leave, but Dara grabbed my arm. "Not so fast."

Shrugging off her hand, I glared at her.

"It has come to my knowledge that you are involved in a business dealing with a known criminal."

"Business dealing? You're nuts."

"If not business, then what? The evidence I have says you either are working with Hagen Lykaios or it's something personal. Care to clarify?"

I peeked at Adrian again.

"Don't look to him. Today he learned what kind of sister you truly are." She threw a set of pictures on her desk, some falling on the floor in front of me.

They were pictures of me sitting on the veranda of Hagen's new restaurant. There was one in particular with Hagen's hand covering mine as we stared into each other's eyes. Then there was another of me leaving the club. My face was flushed, but all other outward appearances looked like normal.

"I don't see how these say I'm a traitor or a whore or whatever else you want it to be. I was having lunch with a childhood friend."

"That's where you're wrong." Dara gave me a knowing smile and gestured to Adam, one of her thugs, to hand me a folder.

I opened it and found a document listing company bylaws and clauses.

As I came to a highlighted section, all the blood drained from my face. I looked up at Dara.

"You can't be serious."

"According to the bylaws, to maintain a security clearance in the company, all executives have to adhere to a morality clause. You, my dear, broke several of them." She stepped toward me. "You associated with someone known for moral turpitude."

Dara smirked at the man in the corner, and I felt such anger pulse in my head that I wanted to scream. That bastard had to have been part of this.

"That makes no sense. Neither Hagen nor any of his brothers have been charged with any crimes. Having lunch with him hasn't broken any bylaw."

"Your association with Hagen Lykaios puts a cloud

around any business this company conducts. He is well known for his association with the unsavory element of Las Vegas. No matter how he cleans himself up, he is still tainted by that world. And those pictures show you are way more than just a family friend as you say."

There was a hard edge to her tone, almost as if she was jealous. I shook that thought from my mind and focused on her craziness.

"It has also come across my desk that we are in negotiations with a major liquor distributor for the next batch of our European elderflower exports."

Yeah, my fucking company, bitch.

"I will not have any of your antics taint the contract." She glared at me as she leaned against the front of her desk. "From my research, the CEO of the company is very selective and she will only recommend companies that meet their criteria of excellence."

It took all my willpower not to blow my cover and tell her the contract negotiations were terminated as of now. When I'd drawn up the contracts for Kipos to be the supplier of elderflower for PSK Distilleries, I was hoping to give Kipos a boost in revenue for the upcoming year so when Adrian took over, the shareholders would see the success he could make of the company.

Hell would freeze over before I gave the contract to Dara.

"I'm the one who's in discussions for the contract. They will only work with me. If it wasn't for me, Kipos wouldn't have been even a contender for the bid."

She waved her hand. "You view your importance a bit too high. I'm sure the head of PSK will see working with the CEO of Kipos a better fit."

"I wouldn't bet on it," I mumbled.

Dara heard me, and the scowl on her face grew angry. "It is my call as the head of the company to make the decision on how we conduct business."

"Meaning?"

"It is time you stepped aside. I won't have you tainting Adrian's future."

"You've got to be kidding. I've brought in more business than any other executive in this company." I turned to Adrian. "Are you seriously listening to this?"

A look passed in his eyes that I couldn't honestly read, but I only hoped he was going along with this to trap Dara.

"I don't have much say in this, Penny. Mom is making some valid points. You should know better than to get involved with Hagen. Implied underworld activity is just as dangerous to future prospects as directly working with convicted criminals."

"What? But you..." I trailed off, taking a step back, and tried to clear the confusion clouding my mind. "Adrian, you believe this bullshit?"

"Yes. Mom should handle all new business at this level."

Was he really siding with Dara?

The back of my throat burned with tears as I tucked a stray hair behind my ear and tried to keep the overwhelming sense of sadness from washing over me.

That was when I saw Adrian twirling the pen he liked to have on him at all times. I stared into his eyes and saw a slight lift of his brow. Relief washed over me. He was playing a part. He wasn't turning on me.

Then a frown and irritation crossed his face. Okay, he was pissed that I'd thought he'd betrayed me. He was going to let me have it later. I deserved it for doubting him, even for half a second.

"Don't try to appeal to Adrian. He has no say in this. I've already spoken to the board. They agree with my decision."

"So, in other words, you're firing me."

"She's finally caught on. For a Stanford graduate, I expected you to see the light sooner. You are no longer employed by Kipos International. You need to hand over all company electronics, including your phone and laptop."

"Wait a second. I need time to remove all my personal information and files from the computers."

"Company equipment is not for personal use. You

forgo any privacy the second you break company regulations."

Well, fuck. Where was a scrambler when I needed one?

"Penny," Adrian said in a low voice and walked up to me, taking my hand.

He slipped a small metal object in my palm. I knew what it was without looking at it. Relief washed over me as I took the device that would wipe my computer's hard drive as soon as I set it against my laptop.

"Fine." I released a breath. "I'll leave. Will you come over later so we can talk?"

"Instead of wasting time talking, I suggest packing. You have three days to move out of the apartment provided to you as an employee of Kipos."

"Now wait just a minute." Adrian faced Dara. "Where do you expect her to live?"

"Not our problem."

Adrian opened his mouth to argue but shut it when I shook my head.

I'd always known when I'd moved into the company townhouse that it was a risk to get attached. This was why I'd spent so much time at the house my parents had built. The property belonged to Adrian and me per Papa's will. Dara could use it, but she would never have any authority over it. The only problem with moving into the house was that I'd never know when Dara would show up or if she would have the place bugged when I wasn't home. And I couldn't expect Adrian to constantly come home to scan the place when he had a full course load and a full-time job.

"Adrian, I'll be fine. I'll stay with friends until I find a place." I opened my shoulder bag and reached inside, pressing the device against the hard drive of my laptop, and pulled it out. "Here. I won't need this anymore."

Adam walked up to me, but instead of handing it to him, I let it drop to the floor, causing a few pieces of the computer to break free.

"You did that on purpose," Adam barked. "That's damaging company property."

I shrugged. "Then have me fired. Oh, wait. That already happened."

"Under that wimpy demeanor, you always were a bitch," he muttered.

"Yep. And it's only going to get more obvious." I glared at Dara as I walked out of the room and toward the elevators.

I wasn't going to even attempt to go to my office. Jeffery knew where I hid all the critical company files in my cabinets and would get them to me.

It took me a few minutes after exiting Kipos headquarters for the haze to set in.

What had just happened? Had Adrian orchestrated this whole thing?

Adrian's words echoed in my mind. *"All I ask is that you trust me."*

Dammit, Adrian, what the hell are you up to?

Did he have any idea what havoc Dara could cause the company without me in the picture? I was going to wring his neck when I got him alone.

That would have to wait; right now it looked like I had to find a place to live. My best friend, Amelia, a former MMA fighter and now international sports promoter, lived in Greece, and moving overseas wasn't an option. My only other real option was my cousin Henna, but she worked for Collin Lykaios and lived in his mega hotel until her new house was complete. I knew she would give me a place to stay without question, but I couldn't see myself living in a hotel run by the very man who threw out his sons without a backward glance.

As I reached my car, my personal phone beeped. It was a message from Adrian.

Adrian: Go find Hagen, he'll give you a place to stay.

Penny: I don't think that's a good idea.

Adrian: It's not like you could lose your job if you're seen associating with him. You already got fired.

Penny: You think you're so funny.

I laughed to myself, shaking my head and opening the door of my car before slipping behind the wheel.

Adrian: I bet you're smiling.

Penny: Yes, I am. Answer a question for me.

Adrian: Go ahead. I have a feeling I know what you want to ask.

Penny: Why did you have me fired?

Adrian: Let me go somewhere private and then I'll call you. It's better to talk than text.

As I waited, I pulled out of the parking garage and headed down the road to my soon-to-be-empty apartment. I wasn't going to even think about staying there anymore. I'd rather get a hotel room. At least there I'd have the comfort of knowing my privacy was ensured.

The second my phone rang, I pushed the Bluetooth speaker to answer the call and greeted Adrian with, "Start explaining."

He groaned. "Well, hell. I didn't expect you to be so pissed."

"I'm waiting." I had the urge to tap my foot but resisted, since it would only cause me to speed and then I'd risk being pulled over.

"Penny, think about it. If you give someone enough rope, she will hang herself. Mom thinks she has me underhand. She doesn't realize I'm on to her need to control the company and our inheritance. Money has always been her motivator. I've known since I was in first grade that she got pregnant on purpose with me to land Papa."

"And what does this have to do with me being unemployed?"

"You aren't unemployed." I could almost see his frown. "The goal is for her to go against Papa's will and then take her down. I'm the only one in position to do it. I also have access to areas you never had. Like her office and private meeting room."

"And how will she go against Papa's will?"

"The will states that a Kipos heir has to hold an executive role at all times. She's already violated it by firing you. That's step one. The next step is for me to catch her funneling money into the offshore account I recently discovered she had."

"Are you saying she's stealing?"

"Is that really a surprise?"

"I guess not. Adrian, I get you're a super sleuth when it comes to finding information, but it has to be completely legal if we want to file any criminal charges against her. If Dara is caught, then she'll use every loophole to get out of the situation."

"Already on it. That is why if you listen to me, my plan will work."

I released a sigh. He was right.

"So, what am I supposed to do in the meantime?"

"You're kidding, right? How about expanding that liquor empire of yours? I hear a certain Lykaios brother is very vested in your success. So vested that he has quite a few businesses designed around it."

The thought of Hagen made my stomach jump. Why would he go out of his way to design a club around Firewater?

"Did you have something to do with Hagen using Firewater as the signature liquor for his clubs and restaurants?"

"I was as surprised as you were. I didn't discover it until I went to a walkthrough session and saw the private tasting room for the various varieties of whiskey and saw all six types of Firewater on the menu."

How long had Hagen known about my business? As far as the world knew, Firewater was owned by a reclusive billionaire who lived in the Maldives.

"Speaking of Hagen—" Adrian broke into my thoughts.

"What?"

"Isn't it time you scratch that itch you've had for him since you were a kid? He wants you. You want him. Plus now Mommy Dearest doesn't have any say in it."

"Get serious. He isn't the commitment-type of guy. I won't be a notch on his bedpost."

"Think about it this way. He can be a notch on *your*

bedpost. If you go in knowing it has a timeline, then no one gets hurt."

The fact I'd thought the same thing over and over throughout the previous night wasn't something I planned to share with my baby brother.

"My sex life is not up for discussion. At this moment in time, I have to pack my shit and then find a decent hotel for the next few nights. I've been evicted, or did you forget? And with the six trade shows in town, I'll be lucky to get an hourly motel."

"It's handled."

"Meaning?"

"Meaning, I just sent a message to Hagen. He says you can have an apartment at the Ida. He'll have the access card waiting for you at his office there."

Before I could respond, Adrian said in a frustrated voice, "Don't you dare argue about this. For once will you let me take care of you? You don't have to take the lead in every damn thing. I arranged a place to stay. I didn't arrange for you to marry him."

I could almost see the irritation on Adrian's face.

"Fine. I'll head to Ida now. But this is only temporary."

CHAPTER SIX

Penny

A LITTLE BIT BEFORE NOON, I pulled into the driveway of Ida. It had taken me longer than I expected to arrange movers and pack my suitcases with enough clothes and necessities to last me until all my personal items could be transported to the apartment Hagen would lend me.

I was estimating it would take me about two weeks to find a decent apartment. Preferably one close to the warehouse where my labs resided.

I wondered how much an apartment in one of Ida's towers went for. Probably in the millions.

Would I offend Hagen if I offered to pay him rent for the next few weeks?

More than likely. Even with all their modern ways and business practices, the Lykaios brothers were Greek, and Greek men had a very traditional view when it came to those they were vested in.

An attendant approached, eying the car. With a smile, I handed him my keys and walked through the doors of Ida. The second I stepped through the threshold, I was struck by the beauty of the interior.

A giant glass sculpture greeted every visitor with an array of colors that mesmerized. The clean lines and muted tones of the rest of the lobby's decor gave the hotel an edgy modern vibe. I had no doubt that Zack had built this property with Hagen in mind. It was refined, yet had the aura of something wicked hidden around some corner. Something that made the visitor seek out the danger.

The reception area was empty with the exception of a few employees working on tablets. The hotel would open to the public in a few weeks, and rumor had it they were already booked to capacity for almost a year out.

The only parts operating were the casinos and shows, which had made their debut last month. I'd missed the invitation-only casino opening celebration because of a last-minute trip to India. Hopefully, nothing would come up, and I could attend the hotel opening in a few weeks.

There was a light scent of sugar and baked goods in the air, making my insatiable craving for sweets wake from its slumber. If there was something I couldn't resist, it was yummy baked goodness. I followed my nose and came to a patisserie. There were cases after cases of any and every type of dessert one could imagine. And to my surprise, there was my personal favorite, *kataifi*. It was made with a special type of pastry that looked similar to angel hair pasta. There was a nutty center hidden within the strands and a sweet sticky syrup. What I wasn't expecting was that it had a whipped layer of sweet cream custard on top, the same way my grandmother, *Yia Yia* Ana, would make it.

Just as I was about to break down and buy a piece of the baked heaven, a man approached me.

"Ms. Kipos, I'm Damian Riker, Ida's general manager. Mr. Lykaios said he's waiting for you in the Diávolos Lounge."

I lifted a brow. "Hagen has a lounge at the hotel called the Devil's Lounge?"

A smile tugged at Damian's lips. "It was actually Mr. Pierce Lykaios's idea. Let's say only two of the three brothers thought the name choice was fitting for the man who would reside on the property."

I could almost see the glare on Hagen's face. No matter how he owned the fact people referred to him as the devil of the Lykaios brothers or Master of Sin or another of a multitude of names, it was apparent he hated people labeling him with his past. Well, it was apparent to me, anyway.

"If you would follow me, I can lead you to the lounge."

I nodded, following Damian down a marble-covered pathway. All the casinos in Vegas were built like mazes with something or another to distract you along the way.

As we passed a section of ultra-high-end retail, I noticed a sign for the botanical gardens.

I hesitated for a second. I was obsessed with nature, especially gardens and wanted to take a peek inside, but I didn't want to seem rude and make Hagen wait.

Damian must have seen my indecision and said, "Would you like to spend a few minutes looking at the gardens? Mr. Lykaios said to walk you through it if you were interested."

"I can do it on my own. Just give me directions to the lounge. I can find my own way there once I'm done."

He hesitated for a second and then nodded, giving me the directions. "If you get lost, here's my card. It has my direct number on it."

I smiled and made my way to the garden.

The first thing I noticed when I entered was the balmy heat of the space and the intoxicating scent of fertile soil and plants. This was my kind of heaven, nature at its finest. There were areas partitioned to keep different species of flowers and organisms from vastly different regions of the world from cross-pollinating.

For the next twenty minutes, I lost myself in the world of botanical beauty.

When I made my way to the lounge, it was nothing like I expected. There wasn't even a sign giving any indication anything was in the area beside a large, overly bulked-up guard. He wore a tailored suit and had his arms crossed, displaying his tree-trunk arms. This was the exact type of guy Dara loved to have waiting on her at any given time.

I approached him with a smile but he scowled.

"Are you lost?" he asked in a "why are you wasting my time?" voice.

"I'm Penny Kipos. Hagen is expecting me. I was told I'd find him here."

"If that were true, Mr. Lykaios would have informed me. Go make an appointment with his secretary like everyone else."

"If you contact Hagen, he will clear me."

"Not happening, lady. Mr. Lykaios doesn't like to be disturbed. Now I suggest you run along."

What the fuck? I wasn't some harpy who wanted to get Hagen.

Well maybe I was, but Hagen had invited me to find him.

"You've got to be kidding me."

"Did I stutter?" He stepped toward me, towering his six-and-a-half-foot height over me. "Get lost, sweetheart. Mr. Lykaios is busy."

My temper was at an all-time high. I was used to Dara treating me like shit, and I'd taken it from her for Adrian's sake, but I would never, ever take it from anyone else again. My days of letting assholes make me feel worthless were over.

"You know what? I'll take care of this with a quick phone call."

"Go right ahead."

"I hope you have a new job lined up." I pulled out my phone and dialed Hagen's number. It might have been better to call Damian, but instinct said Hagen was the better choice.

"Starlight. I was expecting you." The smooth rasp of his voice sent a shiver down my spine and eased my irritation from moments earlier.

"I got caught up in the garden. It's an Eden."

"It was meant to be enjoyed by someone who appreciates it. Are you finished smelling the flowers?"

"Yes, but I have a problem."

"I'm listening."

"The overgrown ape you have guarding access to the lounge just told me to get lost."

"Did he now." His tone grew cold. "I'll take care of it."

"Thank you."

"One thing before I let you go."

"Yes?"

"Go inside with an open mind. You never know, you might like what you see."

That was a strange request.

"I'll do my best," I said and slid my phone back in my purse.

The next thing I knew, the asshole was touching his earpiece and listening to something. His face turned ashen, and he looked at me with worry.

Yes, dickhead, you're in trouble.

After the bouncer pulled his hand back from his ear, he watched me with a bit of fear as sweat beaded his forehead.

What had Hagen said to him?

"I apologize, Sta...Ms. Kipos. I'm sure you understand my need to protect the boss."

I lifted a brow. "Sure. I look like the type of woman who sneaks into a bar so I can seduce the owner."

He didn't comment as he touched his ear again but moved aside and opened a heavy false wall to let me pass.

I stepped into a dimly lit hallway. The distant sound of music echoing told me the lounge was strategically designed to be an invitation only.

I turned the corner and gasped. This was like no

lounge I'd ever encountered. The room was filled with couples and groups enjoying cocktails and food, but what surprised me was the way they were dressed. Women were clad in everything from gowns to barely there lingerie. The men wore a similar variety from three-piece suits to Speedos.

I'd read about places like this in novels and on the Internet but never thought I'd see the inside of one in my life.

Was this Hagen's way of implying this was what I'd get if I accepted his conditions?

My heartbeat accelerated, and my cleft grew damp at the mere thought of it.

I hadn't even seen the main attraction of the place, and I was aroused. I took a set of stairs up to another level.

There were rooms discreetly set to give an illusion of privacy, except for the tables and chairs to provide optimal viewing of the action in the rooms.

My skin tingled. There was a layer of hedonism in the air, and I couldn't help myself—I walked to the farthest room to begin my voyeurism.

I spent the next few minutes perusing the rooms, lost in the fantasies created for the audience to enjoy.

The music blared, and the couples all around me brought visions of what it would be like to be in those positions with Hagen. His hard tattooed body controlling my pleasure, controlling my need, controlling me.

The room that drew my attention the longest held a submissive kneeling before her Dom as he stroked her hair. When he lifted her chin, there was nothing but adoration on her face. They both wore wedding bands, telling me they were more to each other than Dom and submissive.

He offered her his hand, and she rose to stand. He led her to the center of the room where, from the ceiling, a long rope hung with two cuffs attached. The Dom took the submissive's hands and attached them to the restraints. Her skin flushed as if she knew only pleasure awaited her.

A drop of sweat slid down my spine, and the hum of need pulsing between my legs grew to a painful ache.

The couple was so in sync that it was as if he knew her cravings before she did. He pulled out a length of rope from a nearby bag and began to weave it around her body. Layer after layer twined around each breast, making her nipples the only thing exposed. Then he started to work on the rest of her body. He created an intricate pattern that made her look like a flower opening, arms and legs wide. Then with a few precise knots and tugs, he had her hanging from the ceiling. Her knees were drawn up and splayed in the Dom's direction. She was utterly exposed but only to him.

The look in the Dom's eyes and the erection pressing

against his tight jeans told me he was beyond aroused for his submissive.

A moan of longing nearly escaped my lips when the Dom began to finger his sub, and she orgasmed.

The next thing I knew, the Dom walked up to the window and darkened the glass separating the club patrons from him and his submissive.

I released a deep breath and turned to find Hagen leaning against a nearby wall, watching me with the same look of lust that covered the Dom's face.

"I see you found a scene you enjoy." His voice was thick and raspy, making me want to clench my thighs.

"Is there someplace we can talk alone?" I managed to get out breathlessly, giving away how I was feeling after watching the scene.

He studied me. His bright sapphire gaze burned into mine like flames. It took all my strength not to look away.

"Follow me." He offered me his hand.

I slid my palm over his and could swear I felt a shock of energy that coursed through every nerve in my body.

He led me to an empty hallway and scanned his eye against a retinal panel, causing the door to open.

We entered what I could only describe as a control room. There were monitors showing every aspect of the club covering two walls, a giant desk with stacks of papers and another table with three computers.

"This is where you work?"

A grin touched his lips. "This belongs to one of my partners. I technically am no longer part of the kink club's infrastructure."

"Technically?"

"Yes. I'm an upstanding citizen now. My vices are nightclubs, restaurants, and Vegas shows."

"Do you partake in these clubs?"

He lifted a brow. "Occasionally. Why? Are you offering to be my submissive?"

Heat flooded my cheeks at the thought of being on my knees for Hagen and letting him command my body.

"Perhaps." I tried to play it cool, but there was no way to hide how much I wanted him.

"Adrian tells me you need a place to stay." He moved in front of the desk and leaned back against it while folding his sculpted, tattooed arms across his body.

Holy fuck, why did he have to be so mouthwatering?

I shook my thoughts back and focused on the task I was here for. "Yes. Dara found out we met for lunch and fired me." I paused. "She said I was engaged in activities that went against the moral code of the company."

"How is a lunch immoral? Besides, the only people who know what happened in the office are you and me."

The flush on my face intensified as did the desire for

the man who'd given me my first non-self-administered orgasm.

Thankfully my voice remained calm when I said, "Apparently she had a clause put into the bylaws around the time of my father's death that stated executives are not allowed to engage in activities or associate with anything or anyone who has questionable businesses or practices."

"And yet you still came and sought me out. Are the answers worth the risk?"

"Yes. The company belongs to Adrian, and I will be damned if I'll let Dara take his inheritance from him or hurt him in the process."

He stood and walked toward me until he was barely a few inches from me. He trailed his fingers up my arms, making goosebumps prickle my skin.

"So you're willing to accept my stipulations for helping you?"

My breath began to come out a bit shallow and my heartbeat drummed into my ears.

Here goes, Penny. Time to do something reckless.

I set my hand on his chest, holding in a moan of desire. "I told you I was willing without the stipulation of your help."

He grabbed my hand and moved it to the front of his pants, on top of his hard, thick length. "Be sure, Starlight.

Once I take you, there's no going back. You will be mine until this heat between us burns out."

My mouth dried up, but I couldn't help but squeeze his cock. "I'm sure."

"I will fuck you whenever and wherever I want. You will do everything I tell you to do. Which includes many of the things you saw in the club."

I rubbed my fingers up and down his denim-covered length. "Are you trying to convince me to change my mind? Do you think the idea of kink frightens me?"

A groan escaped his lips, and his breath grew shallow. "Fuck. I should do the right thing and send you packing, but I'm a selfish man and have wanted you longer than I can remember."

I stared into his hypnotic gaze, swallowing to wet my parched throat, and then asked, "Does it look like I'm complaining?"

"Starlight, you have no idea what you're getting into. I won't give you false expectations of what will happen between us."

"Then make it clear and see what happens," I challenged, giving his length a hard stroke.

"You won't ever get nice and sweet from me." He cupped my throat, squeezed, and then slid his palm down the column of my neck and into the open collar of my shirt. "It will be raw, untamed, and dirty. I am as depraved and dark as the world believes. Especially when it comes to sex."

My core clenched.

"I want it dirty," I responded, feeling my nipples pebble as his pupils dilated.

I'd spent my life living for others, now I took what I wanted even if it had a finite timeframe. No matter what happened, I'd never regret choosing this step.

I squeezed up and down the length of his engorged cock. Hagen closed his eyes for a second, enjoying the feel of my fingers.

"I want it untamed."

I circled the head of his length with my fingertip.

"I want it raw." I pressed my body against him, trapping my hand between us.

"You may end up regretting this." He paused, gripping my hair and tugging my head back.

"It's a risk I'm willing to take."

"You have a deal." He slammed his lips against mine.

Immediately, the desire I'd felt for this man burst free. I met his mouth's demands with my own. The kiss we'd shared at his lounge was nothing compared to this. The taste of him exploded in my mouth, bourbon with a hint of orange. His kiss was all consuming and primal. It was as if he was starved to taste me and now that he had, he would consume all of me. His tongue rolled against mine, causing a low moan to escape my lips.

I knew it would be like this. My body burned for him, and all we'd done so far was kiss. My breasts swelled against the confines of my bra, and my clit throbbed.

I lifted my arms around his shoulders, letting him walk me back until my ass hit the edge of the large desk.

"God, you're perfect." He lifted his hand to my waist, pulling my top over my head and discarding my bra, and then slid his palm under the swell of my breast, squeezing the mound while pinching the tip with his index finger and thumb.

"More." I gasped as I began to unbutton his shirt. The feel of his callused hand was like lightning firing all along my skin. My body ached for more. My nipples ached for more. Hell, my pussy was dying for more.

He released my mouth for only long enough to rid himself of his shirt before he was back, devouring me.

If his drugging kisses were something I was already addicted to, then what would happen once he fucked me?

I'd find out my answer soon enough.

He shimmied my skirt over my hips as he set me on the edge of the desk and settled himself between my legs. His thick, hard cock rubbed against my soaked slit, and all I could do was throw my head back as my pussy spasmed, wanting nothing more than him filling me.

His breath was coming in hard pants as if he were running a marathon, and his eyes blazed with untamed need.

His thumb hooked onto the sides of my panties, and in one swift pull, my underwear was history. "I promise next time we'll go slower, but I need to be inside you. I've dreamed about you clamping down on me for too long and through too many fantasies."

He pulled his wallet out of his back pocket and fished for a condom. I watched him as he freed his enormous cock from his pants. A pang of worry crept in. This was so going to hurt.

He must have seen my reaction because he stopped, closing his eyes for a second.

"We can stop any time, Starlight," he gritted out.

My heart skipped a beat, knowing he would stop for me. He had the world fooled, but not me.

Instead of responding, I wrapped my fingers around his steel length, pumping up and down while taking his hand and pressing it against my swollen folds. "I don't want to stop. I want you to make this ache between my legs go away."

A flash of surprise entered his eyes and was quickly replaced with fire. He circled my clit over and over until I was on the verge of madness and then right when I was about to go over, he pressed his sheathed cock into my sopping pussy.

Immediately, I braced myself for the invasion and the pain.

"God, you're so tight," he said through clenched teeth. "How long has it been for you?"

He pulled out a fraction and pushed all the way in, making me stiffen and bite my lip.

"Fuck," I gasped. "That hurt more than I thought it would."

Maybe I should have told him I was a virgin. No, it was better this way.

Hagen froze and stared down at me. "Why didn't you tell me?"

"Because I knew you wouldn't go through with it." I tried to shift to bring him deeper, but he gripped my hips.

"Starlight," he whispered, dropping his forehead to mine. "Your first time shouldn't be like this. And especially not with me."

I cupped his face. "I've wanted you since I was a kid. It's only right that you're my first."

There was raw emotion in his gaze, making me lift my face to kiss him.

"Hagen?"

"Yes."

"You can move now."

A smile touched his lips. "Yes, ma'am."

He pulled all the way out, leaving only the crest of his cock inside my channel and then slammed back in.

I cried out as the pain disappeared and was replaced by a deep-seated need.

CHAPTER SEVEN

Hagen

I WAS SO GOING to hell, and I couldn't care less.

She'd given me her virginity and had no clue what that meant. She was mine. I'd wanted her for far too long to turn back now.

Her wet pussy clamped around my cock, and it took all my strength not to come on the spot.

I lifted her into my arms and carried her to the large sofa in the corner of the room, making sure my cock stayed buried deep in her heat.

This was definitely not how her first time was supposed to be, but I'd do my damnedest to make this good for her. She deserved to be seduced, to be cherished, to be loved by a man worthy of her.

Why the fuck she chose me made no sense. My hands had done unspeakable things, and she wanted them on her.

"Why me?" I asked again as I lowered her back and slowly positioned myself over her.

She tightened her thighs around my waist, sucking me deeper inside her body. "Because you're the only man I've ever wanted this badly."

Fuck, this woman was going to destroy me, and we'd only started...whatever it was that was going on between us.

"You keep saying things like that, and I'm going to keep you."

I lowered my mouth and latched on to one of her full, swollen breasts, then worried the straining bud with my tongue and teeth.

The gasps and moans escaping her lips were pushing me to the point where I'd lose control. There was no way a man could be expected to hold back when he was balls-deep inside his dream girl.

I sounded like a pussy, but I didn't give a fuck.

My dick pulsed inside her, screaming for me to move, to pummel her tight cunt. Instead, I gave her slight shifts of my cock, just enough to give her the release she needed before I let the animal raging inside me loose.

She rolled her hips and my eyes nearly crossed. I was in deep shit.

"Where the fuck did you learn to do that?" I asked through clenched teeth.

Her cheeks flushed as she looked away.

I captured her jaw, bringing her face back to me, and at the same time I pulled out to the tip and thrust back in.

Her body bowed, and her legs tightened.

"What embarrassing things have you been doing?"

Her fingers gripped my shoulders, but she remained quiet.

My palm slid to her throat and squeezed. Her eyes immediately dilated, and her pussy contracted.

"I read a lot of books, and I watch..." She trailed off, making me smile. "Forget I said the last part."

Oh no, she wasn't going to get away with hiding.

"Watch what? Porn?"

She bit her lip and nodded.

"You definitely aren't the naive girl you like the world to see. I like that. You're an enigma." I took her mouth and whispered against her lips, "But know this—now that you're mine, I plan to corrupt you in ways you've never imagined."

My words caused her pussy to grow damper and little spasms to flutter around my cock. "You like that."

"Yes." Her nails dug into my arms, leaving no doubt I'd have marks. "I want you to teach me everything."

I stared into her green gaze, trying to see if she meant what she was saying. What I saw was desire and a need she was desperate to explore.

Fuck. She was really giving me all of her.

I was definitely going to hell. No sane man would say no to her, especially after feeling her slick, swollen cunt wrapped around his cock.

"From this moment on, you're mine. Is that clear? It won't end until the fire burns out between us."

She nodded and then rolled her hips again, making me clench my teeth.

"Fuck, you are way too good at that move."

"Hagen, I need you to stop talking and make love to me. And I don't want it soft and gentle. Fuck me like you mean it."

I lifted a brow. This woman was a constant surprise. "If I fuck you the way I want, you won't be able to walk. How about you let me decide how this goes."

I pulled out and slammed back in. She gasped and tightened her hold around my body.

"Hagen, please."

"I've got this, baby. All you have to do is enjoy."

I slid my hand between our bodies until I reached her soaked core and the bundle of nerves I knew would send her over. The first stroke of my fingers had her writhing under me. The second had her biting my shoulder.

Her cries pushed my need until all I could think about was both of us coming together. My thrusts grew harder and uncoordinated as I rubbed her clit.

"Yes, oh God, yes." She threw her head back as her pussy milked my cock, clamping hard, and her nails raked my back.

Her orgasm was the most beautiful sight I'd ever seen. Skin flushed, gaze wild, and screams filled with ecstasy.

Before I knew it, my control snapped, and I followed, coming so hard I saw stars.

Penny

MY BREATH HAD BARELY CALMED when Hagen's phone began to ring. It went to voicemail but started up again almost immediately.

"Shit. I have to get that. It's probably one of my managers." Hagen lifted his head, searching my eyes, but didn't say anything more. After a few seconds, he shifted, pulling free of my body, and rose off the sofa.

I gasped, missing the sense of fullness I'd felt only moments before.

"Stay right there. I'll be right back."

Hagen tugged on his pants and went to an attached bathroom. When he returned, he knelt in front of me and cleaned me with a warmed washcloth.

"Don't you have to call your manager?" I tried to sit up, closing my eyes against the ache between my legs, and the embarrassment I felt at him wiping the tinge of blood from my folds.

"Relax. It's my job to take care of you. My manager can wait." A smile tugged his lips. "Besides, I know you like me touching you."

My cheeks heated further. He was right. It was a unique mix of pleasure and pain, something I could definitely get used to.

"Now let me see who's calling." Hagen rose to his feet, threw the washcloth in the hamper near the bathroom door, and then moved to his desk.

I watched him as he dialed a number on his phone and began to speak in a low tone. A crease formed between his brows but eased as he glanced at me.

I couldn't believe it had actually happened. I'd slept with Hagen Lykaios. For the first time in my life, my dream came true.

The giddiness ebbed as I realized I had no idea what

would happen next. I had no doubt Hagen would keep his word of helping me find out the truth behind Papa's death. The question was how was I going to handle a sexual relationship with him without losing myself in the process.

I could handle this. My time with Hagen would be something I could look back on and say I didn't hide away as everyone expected and stepped into a world of adventure.

Maybe Adrian was right. It was time I did something for myself, and that included Hagen Lykaios. This was my opportunity to go public with my endeavors without the worry of repercussions.

A pang of guilt had me sighing. Dara was entirely in charge of Kipos, and I had no way of keeping an eye on her. I had to admit Kipos wasn't where I saw myself in the future. And Adrian had made it clear he didn't want the company either. The only hope I had was a buyout, but then Papa's legacy would end.

I shook the thoughts of Kipos aside and opened my lids. My gaze collided with piercing blue ones across the room, and the hum of arousal from a few moments ago ignited.

Hagen watched me with caution, as if he thought with one false move I'd run. His shirtless body was a work of art, corded abs leading to a sexy V that disappeared into the waistband of his jeans. The tattoos on his arms added to his bad-boy image.

He was a walking Greek god. A god of sin, of decadence, of indulgence, everything a good girl was warned to stay away from—everything I couldn't wait to experience.

He finished his conversation, set his phone down, and then walked over to me, crouching in front of me.

His palms glided up my naked thighs until they settled on my hips. I gripped his shoulders, needing to touch him. He cupped my face and kissed my forehead. "Starlight, are you okay?"

"I'm not sure what happens next." I leaned into him.

"Neither do I. This is all new territory for me."

I pulled back and frowned. "Hagen, you've had more than your share of women. I doubt that you don't know how to handle me."

"That's it. You're not like other women. I don't want to handle you." He peered at me.

"What does that mean?"

"The choice is yours. I will give you a place to stay and help you find out the truth behind your father's death no matter what you decide."

"I still don't understand. Don't you want me?"

"God, you have no idea how much I want you. I want you more than any other woman I've ever encountered."

His fingers flexed on my waist. "What I'm trying to say is that you don't have to sleep with me as we bargained. My help comes free and clear. I only want you in my bed if you want to be there."

The longing he failed to hide in his words made my heart ache. Hagen was definitely nothing like his reputation. I knew it was all a facade.

I moved forward, pushing Hagen back onto the floor before straddling him, my exposed pussy flush against his lower abdomen. There was a pang of discomfort, but the heat of his body was well worth the pain.

"Does this tell you what I want?"

"Starlight." His voice was gruff. "I know I asked you this before, but I have to be sure. Do you understand what you're getting into with me? No matter what you believe, I've done everything the rumors say and may have to continue some of them. Being with me will give you a reputation, one I'm not sure you can handle."

"What if I told you I'm not the innocent you believe me to be?"

"Baby, up until twenty minutes ago, you were a virgin. That's as innocent as it gets."

"Outside of my sex life, I'm involved in a lot more than you could ever know. I've just mastered keeping a low profile." Before he could say anything, I added, "I want it all, Hagen. Corrupt me as you said you would earlier. I dare you."

He sighed. His fingers glided up my spine and gripped my hair. "You asked for it."

He covered my mouth with his, sealing the deal. Heat began to grow in my core as the ache of need began to grow again. Hagen's hands covered my breasts, squeezing the mounds, and a low moan escaped my lips.

At that moment Hagen's phone rang again, and he groaned against my lips.

"We have to go."

"Okay," I said, rising to my feet with Hagen's help. My cheeks heated as I noticed my arousal on his stomach. He followed my gaze and smiled, swiping a finger through the wetness and bringing my essence to his lips.

"Delicious."

I shook my head and quietly dressed.

After both of us were ready, I picked up my handbag and waited.

He took my hand in his and led me out of the room and toward a set of doors I hadn't seen earlier. As we passed other members of the club, we garnered some curious looks.

I glanced down at myself and knew I looked out of place. My thigh-high boots and minidress, though edgy and fashion-forward in the outside world, clashed with the elegant, yet scantily clad women all around me. I held in the urge to tug at my dress, feeling a bit self-conscious. They were all beautiful in their own right, and whether with a partner or not, they fit.

"Don't," Hagen said as he continued through a door and down a long hallway.

"Don't what?"

"Don't compare yourself to the women out there."

"How would you know what I was thinking?"

"I can feel the energy around you. If you want to know why they're staring at you, it's because I never participate in the club. And having you on my arm has them curious."

"So you're not into kink as you made me believe?"

He glanced over his shoulder and smirked. "I didn't say that. I like to dominate, but I don't need all the extras. Those are Pierce's things, that's why he built this place. It's a safe place for like-minded individuals."

Well, I never expected that. I would never have guessed Pierce was into BDSM, but then again, I'd always viewed him as the big brother who watched out for me. Plus, the fact he'd had a relationship with my best friend Amelia made it seem weird to think of them doing the whips-and-nipple-clamps thing. And for Zack, there was no telling what he was into. He was the most unpredictable of all of them. If anyone was into the kink side of things, it was probably him.

I needed to get my mind away from this train of thought, or I'd throw up.

"The last thing I truly want to think about is Pierce or Zack's sexual escapades. That's just gross. They're family."

Hagen stopped, turned around, and crowded me back against a near wall. "What does that make me? They are, after all, my brothers."

"You're my lover." My voice was a bit breathless and needy. "You are in a different realm altogether."

My answer must have pleased him because he kissed the area where my neck and shoulder met and hummed.

We worked our way through the club and out the back doors. When we reached a bank of elevators, Hagen drew out two cards, one black and one red.

"As always, the choice is yours. The black card is for my penthouse, and the red is for your own apartment, on a different floor, far, far away from me."

I knew without a doubt where I wanted to stay. Hagen was my adventure, a side of life I wanted and until now never had the chance to explore.

"Is this a life-altering decision like in *The Matrix*? The blue pill or the red pill?"

A smile tugged at his lips. "You could say that. It's more a choice of corruption or innocence."

I moved to take the black one, but he pulled it away before I grasped it.

"If you take this one, you live with me from now on. You will be my woman in public and private. I won't hide who or what you are to me. You will garner a reputation. People will assume you're under my control. There won't be any going back to the way things were between us. I will fuck you, use you, make you mine in every way possible. I'm not the nice man you deserve."

I stood on tiptoes, leaned in to kiss his lips, and pulled the black access card from his fingers.

"I know what I'm getting into, Mr. Lykaios."

CHAPTER EIGHT

Hagen

I STARED at the now-closed elevator door, trying to wrap my mind around the woman who was moving into my penthouse.

Christ. This was actually happening. She was mine, and it had been her choice.

What the fuck had I gotten myself into? How the hell was I going to handle her? She wasn't my usual M.O. I couldn't treat her the way I did other women.

"Was that Penny I saw locking lips with you?" Pierce asked as he came up behind me.

I was not going to answer the obvious. Plus, Pierce was the nosiest of the three of us and would keep bombarding me with questions the second I replied to one.

"Dude. I understand pussy whipped, but damn, man. She's got you by the balls, and I'm not sure if either of you realizes it."

"Fuck off." I pushed past my know-it-all brother and headed to the lobby. "I have a meeting to get to."

"If it's the one with Draco, might as well wait for me. Apparently, he views his assistance with Penny's inquiry as a personal favor to all of us."

This just got better and better. "So Zack's joining us?"

"He's at the bar with Draco and a few of his men right now. They had other business to discuss before we got there."

Now that was another thing I had to worry about.

Zack and Draco were getting chummy. My involvement with the mobster had been about survival. Zack, on the other hand, had no such issues. Whatever he was up to would probably cause all of us grief in the long run.

As of late, everything in Zack's life revolved around getting revenge on Collin for all the shit he put us through. On the top of his list of grievances with Collin was the fact we only learned about our mother's illness a few days before she'd passed. She had battled breast cancer for nearly a year without us being there to care for her. I grieved my mother, but I'd accepted long ago that she chose to stay with Collin even when I'd offered her a way out. Pierce had the same resigned acceptance as I did, but Zack was different.

He was the youngest and closest to Mama in the last years of her life. He was determined to make Collin suffer for tearing our family apart, and the best way to do it was by destroying the Lykaios Holdings empire, one piece at a time.

"Honestly he's got to let this need for revenge go. Collin isn't worth all the effort." I took a path through the maze of the casino that would be the shortest to the cigar bar.

"Preaching to the choir. But then again, we aren't all built with the ability to compartmentalize like you. Outside of Persephone, there isn't a single soul who can incite any feelings from you."

The mention of Starlight's name made me wonder what she was doing upstairs. Was she making herself at home or was she snooping through all the rooms and drawers?

"We are not discussing her. Our arrangement is private and has nothing to do with the matter at hand."

"Yeah right." Pierce paused and faced me. "She's a long-term girl. I don't want you fucking with her emotions. She isn't used to men like us."

I clenched my teeth. "Are you warning me away from her?"

"There isn't a chance in hell that would happen. What I'm saying is if you break her heart, I'll rearrange your face. And I'm positive Zack will join me."

"What if I told you that I planned to keep her?"

Pierce broke out in laughter and started toward the bar again. "She isn't a puppy. She is a flesh-and-blood woman with a mind of her own. You don't own her."

"She knows exactly what she's getting with me."

"I swear talking to you is as effective as talking to a brick wall. All I'm saying is be careful with her. She is gentle and someone who's spent her whole life fitting into a mold that keeps her invisible."

"She isn't as weak as everyone believes." I countered Pierce's statement. "I'm the perfect outlet for her to let loose."

I nodded to the hostess as we walked through the archway of the Erebus Bar. She smiled and studied both Pierce and me with more interest than necessary.

She was new and had no idea that as a rule the Lykaios brothers never got involved with the staff. It was one sure-fire way to fuck up one's business.

"As I said. You break her heart. I break your face."

"Why don't you stop worrying about my love life and focus on the European promoter you can't get over. Rumor has it that her European heavyweight champion could take your guy, hands down."

A scowl formed on his face. "You're an asshole."

"Never said I wasn't."

"And for the record, my boy is the best in the world and can take on any cover model playboy Amelia Nephus has in her arsenal."

I'd touched a nerve. Good. He deserved it after thinking I'd hurt Starlight on purpose. Yes, I'd fuck her, corrupt her, and make her mine for as long as she wanted, but I'd never intentionally hurt her.

"Ahh, there's my boy," Draco Jackson said in an accent that was more Japanese than American.

Draco rarely, if ever, was seen in public. He was virtually born into the Ninkyō Dantai, or more widely known as the Yakuza, the mafia that ruled the underworld of Japan. His father and most of his family were high-level members of one of the ruling clans in the organization.

As a boy barely over the age of eighteen, he was sent to California to expand his family's reach. Instead of settling in LA or San Francisco, he chose to move to Nevada and establish himself in Las Vegas.

He'd changed his name to something "more American" for anonymity and ruled with an iron fist behind the scenes.

Now over half a century later, he had expanded

beyond Vegas to major cities across the US and had a stronghold to rival the organization he'd left in his youth.

The almost-seventy-five-year-old pulled me into a tight bear hug as he whispered in Japanese, *"I hear you have finally captured your Starlight."*

"Captured is not the word I'd use, Oyabun. More like coerced." I responded in fluent Japanese and addressed him with his title as the "boss."

As part of my training at the beginning of my work, Draco insisted I learn multiple languages. Today, outside of the Greek and English that I learned to speak as a baby, I was versed in Chinese, Japanese, Spanish, Italian, and French. All the languages used by major mafia syndicates around the world.

We took our seats, mine being in between Draco and Zack and with Pierce across from us.

We remained quiet as Draco was settled with a drink. He would have to be the first to speak as per the decorum he expected. Though Draco had lived in America, he followed very traditional etiquette for business. The fact he showed open affection for me was an anomaly even his family couldn't understand.

"Before we talk about your Kipos issue, I want to know how the Popov situation went."

I held in a groan. The last thing I wanted to discuss was Mike, but I had no choice.

"It's handled. Popov won't bother you again."

"Excellent." Draco nodded, not asking for further clarification, something I was grateful for.

I'd taken care of Mike, but not in the way Draco expected. At this very moment, Mike Popov was on his way to Russia via a cargo hold and then would be transferred to a work facility run by one of Draco's associates.

Mike would spend his life separated from his daughter, but at least he'd be alive and I wouldn't have more blood on my hands.

"Now to the reason we are here," Draco now said in English. "After our conversation the other day, I learned some interesting things. Jacob Kipos was in the process of changing his will when his car wrapped itself around a tree."

"It is only to be expected, since he was filing for divorce." Zack stirred the olive in his martini.

"I am positive no one knows the changes went through." Draco smiled. "The will that was never made public states Dara would get a stipend for the rest of her life, but the controlling interest for Kipos would be divided between Adrian and Persephone. The only way Dara profits is if the company is sold. Then she will get a lump-sum payout."

"So in other words, Dara had the means to manipulate

the situation in the aftermath of Jacob's death," Pierce added. "That explains why she was so determined to control Penny."

"And why Dara is so determined to sell Kipos to the highest bidder before Adrian turns twenty-one," I added.

Last night when my brothers had decided to visit me, it was to tell me that Kipos International was open to a buyout. The information was presented to select companies, one of them being a company HPZ had acquired a few weeks ago.

"Yes. Now you're catching on. I found—"

"What does this have to do with any of the information related to Jacob Kipos's accident?" Zack asked, cutting off Draco, which resulted in a glare from him.

When it came to Draco, it was well known that respect was a big deal. No one dared to interrupt him. He tolerated my idiot brother because he was still young. But even that had limits, and the last thing I needed was Zack offending Draco.

A pissed-off Draco could mean a world of trouble for us.

"Zacharias, you have the least patience of the three of you. Just like your father. Don't make his mistakes. Money isn't the only power in this world." Draco shook his head at his men who had moved closer to us, seeing his irritation.

"I apologize, sir."

Draco inclined his head, accepting Zack's apology. "Now back to what I was relaying. My second and third lieutenant are personally tracing all the information up to and following the accident."

At that moment, one of Draco's men set folders in front of us.

"Here is a copy of the executed will. I can assume you plan to purchase the company."

None of us either confirmed or denied.

Draco smiled. "Good, keep it quiet. Dara Kipos is a snake waiting to strike, but your job is to be the grey mongoose. Immune to the cobra's venom and ready to tear her apart the second she turns her back."

I released a sigh. It was amazing how the man could come out with some wise but pertinent statement and use animals as examples.

"*Oyabun*, may I ask what you will require in payment for your help?" I held Draco's gaze and saw amusement crinkle his eyes.

"From Pierce—" Draco's attention went to my brother, "—I want ringside seats for the heavyweight bout he is planning to negotiate between his prizefighter and the one signed under Amelia Nephus. Rumor has it you two have unfinished business."

Then his focus moved to Zack. "Outside our earlier discussion, I require access to your property on the island of Bora Bora for my granddaughter's wedding. She told me it was booked out for the next year, but I'm sure you can rearrange some things for her."

"And you." He moved his onyx eyes to me. "I want three cases from the unlabeled reserve your Starlight is hiding from the world. My sources say she is a genius and has created the best batch of her whiskey to date."

All the hairs on my arms stood up. How the fuck had he discovered Starlight's secret? I wouldn't question him. Not now, when my brothers were around. My relationship with Draco was strong, but there was a time and place to challenge him, and this was not it.

"As you wish, *Oyabun*. But I will warn you. It may take some convincing to get her to part with any of that bottling. Especially if no one is supposed to know about it." My tone couldn't hide that I was referring to my brothers.

Draco smirked and continued. "As long as you get them to me before you firstborn arrives, I'll be fine."

Firstborn?

Immediately a vision of Starlight round with our child appeared in my mind.

"What a second." Zack broke into my thoughts. "Are you fucking kidding me? Penny is the reclusive owner of Firewater? Not some overweight, overindulged heiress on an island in the Indian Ocean?"

I kept quiet.

"Now it makes complete sense—the restaurants and the clubs. Damn, asshole, you're obsessed. When she finds out, she is going to have your stalker ass committed. You are seriously one crazy fucker."

Draco cleared his throat, essentially stopping Zack's profanity-laced opinions.

"Are we in agreement, gentlemen?"

Pierce, Zack, and I agreed and then for the next thirty minutes discussed the plans for the opening of the hotel and the party that would take place in a few weeks.

After Draco left via a private access area, I readied myself for an inquisition. But to my surprise, neither Pierce nor Zack said anything. They only stared at me with shit-eating grins on their faces.

"Care to share?" I asked, which only made them laugh out loud.

"Never did I think I'd see the day Hagen Christopher Lykaios would fall. And for a naive little nature nymph." Pierce lifted a glass to me. "This is going to be fun to watch."

"Whatever. Go make a deal with your ex or something."

"How long have you known Penny was the mastermind behind Firewater?" Zack picked up a cigar, lighting it and then taking a few deep puffs.

"A few years now."

"And you didn't think it was important to let us know?" Zack leaned back in his chair. "We could have helped her. Hell, we could have negotiated better deals for the whiskey."

"Or she could have gotten more out of your tightwad ass with a game of cards," Pierce added, resulting in Zack shooting him the bird.

"The point of keeping quiet was so she could do it on her own. She's phenomenal at her job both at Kipos and with PSK Distilleries."

"Shit," Pierce exclaimed. "I should have known that PSK stood for Persephone Starlight Kipos. Damn, she's good. I can't believe she never slipped during one of our monthly poker games."

Poker games. Why the fuck was my woman playing poker with my brothers?

My woman. I liked the sound of that.

"What poker games?"

"The ones you never show up to. She subbed in your place a few times and then became a regular. She's a card shark, by the way. She's cleaned us out too many times to count," Zack added. "I thought I was good, but that girl has a computer for a brain and it's like watching a processor analyze faces, reactions, and tells while keeping a serene facade."

Zack was by far the best poker player I'd ever

encountered. A game of cards and a twenty-million-dollar pot were what launched the beginnings of his real-estate empire.

"By the way, does she know her cover is blown?"

"She only found out I knew yesterday. But I'll have to tell her that Draco and you two doofuses know."

"Like we'd rat her out." Zack sounded offended.

I pushed back from the table and rose.

"Where are you going?" Pierce lifted a brow.

"To see how my new roommate is settling in."

CHAPTER NINE

Penny

SO THIS WAS how the ballers of the world lived.

I sipped my wine and gazed out at the incredible view of the Las Vegas Strip. The lights twinkled like stars, and cars buzzed around, making it seem like a world far away from where I was instead of at the bottom of the building I would now live in.

After I left Hagen gaping in the lobby, I spent twenty minutes trying to decide what to make of my change in circumstances.

I was technically unemployed but technically not. I was technically homeless but not.

Now I was settled into the palatial bedroom I

would share with Hagen and not knowing what to expect. As of this afternoon, my virginity was history, and now I belonged to Hagen, or so he said. Whatever that meant.

If I kept thinking this was all temporary, I wouldn't get sucked in too deep. That was the only way to handle a relationship with any of the Lykaios boys. They weren't the settling-down type.

I had to view this as stepping onto the ride of my life. It would be something I could brag to my children one day about.

No, never mind.

I wasn't ever going to brag about my sexual escapades with any future offspring. Hell, I couldn't even discuss it with Adrian.

Thinking of...why hadn't he called me? I moved to the coffee table where I'd set my phone. However, before I could pick it up, the elevator opened.

I paused, feeling goosebumps prickle my skin.

Hagen stepped off, and immediately my breath hitched. He was so sexy with his disheveled hair and blazing blue eyes.

"Starlight," was all he said as he dropped a large envelope on the coffee table and stalked in my direction. He slid a hand around my waist, capturing my lips in the process.

The kiss was all demand and possession, making my nipples bead and my cleft grow damp.

I wrapped my arms and legs around him as his hands cupped my ass, pressing me against his hard, thick cock.

I pulled back, gasping for air, and breathlessly said, "That's some hello, Mr. Lykaios."

"I try." His fingers flexed under my bottom. "You have the best ass of any woman I've ever seen."

I rolled my eyes. "Okay, I buy that. You're surrounded by pin-up girls."

"They're plastic. I don't do plastic. I have a thing for petite, raven-haired nymphs with curves." To emphasize his words, he pushed me back against the glass wall and rubbed his length up and down my slick cleft.

Tilting my head back, I closed my eyes. "You're good at that."

"Starlight, this is only the beginning." He brought my feet back to the hardwood floor. "Are you sore?"

I felt embarrassment creep into my cheeks. I was tender but not truly sore. The thought of having to wait a day or two to have sex again was out of the question.

"No."

Hagen cocked his head to the side. "I want the truth. I'm not touching you again until I know it won't be painful for you."

I held his gaze and said, "I'm tender but not in pain. I

don't need recovery time. This isn't some Victorian romance where the young virgin can't be touched so soon after losing her innocence."

He shook his head. "Woman, I never know what's going to come out of your mouth."

He released me, walked to the coffee table. "This is for you."

He picked up the envelope and handed it to me.

My head, still in the haze of desire, tried to focus on what he'd given me. "What is it?"

I pulled out the contents of the envelope.

"It's my health report. I get tested every few months. This one was from last week. It's no secret that I have a past. But I wanted you to know I'm clean and I've never had sex without a condom." He ran a hand through his black hair and watched me.

God, I hadn't even thought to ask. Maybe I was as naive as everyone believed. At least there was one of us who had a functioning brain.

"Thank you for this."

"You're welcome."

I tucked the papers back in the envelope and returned them to the table.

"Now what?" I asked, feeling the crackle of energy between us ignite again.

"Now you strip."

I swallowed. "Here? In the living room? But the lights are on, and we're surrounded by windows."

"And we're too high up for the world to see in. I've fantasized about taking you in this room. Tonight, I plan to make fantasy a reality."

"Oh." My heartbeat drummed in my ears as my pussy clenched.

Slowly he came to stand in front of me. His blue gaze was almost black with desire. He lifted his hand and ran a thumb over my lips, down the column of my throat, and between the open collar of my shirt.

Immediately, my body heated.

"Take off your clothes, Starlight."

Licking my parched lips, I held his stare and unbuttoned my blouse. Hagen pushed it from my shoulders and onto the floor.

I reached behind me to unzip my skirt. As with my top, Hagen helped the material pool at my feet.

When I moved to unclasp my bra, Hagen covered my hands with his. "Let me do the rest." His voice was rough and deep, filled with arousal, and the bulge of his cock strained against the seam of his pants. "It's too bad you put on another pair of underwear."

"I can't walk around commando all day."

"Of course you can. From now on, I insist."

The thought of going naked under my skirt made a

pang of uncertainty and arousal course through my body.

As his palms glided around my rib cage to unclasp my bra, his breath teased the skin of my neck, and I couldn't help but tilt toward him.

He smelled so good.

I could have gotten lost in the intoxicating blend of his cologne and his natural essence mixed with the hint of cigars.

"Did you just sniff me?" There was a tinge of humor in his words.

My face heated, and I knew I was probably beet red with embarrassment. "Maybe."

"Good to know you enjoy how I smell." He slowly lowered to the ground and rubbed his nose along the damp seam of my crotch. "Because I sure the hell love the scent of you, especially on that beautiful, innocent pussy of yours."

He gently bit my mound, and a shocking wave of desire spasmed deep in my core.

I braced one hand on the back of the couch to keep my balance while the other gripped his hair.

"I'm not innocent anymore."

"Baby, you're more innocent than you could ever know."

"Then I suggest you corrupt me."

"Believe me, I plan to." His lips curved as his tongue darted out and he licked my fabric-covered pussy.

I arched my head back, loving the erotic sensation.

He gripped the sides of my thong, tore it from my hips, and then threw it over his shoulder.

"God, you are so fucking sexy," he said as he gazed up at me.

Before I could respond, his lips descended on my swollen clit. He sucked and teased the sensitive bud until I was writhing against his mouth. The second my pussy quickened, he plunged his tongue deep. My back bowed as he devoured me.

The sensation was too much.

I tried to pull away, but he held me tight against his unyielding mouth.

"Come, Starlight. Come for me." He plunged a finger deep inside me, curving it against the sensitive bundle of nerves at the top.

"Oh God, Hagen." My body detonated.

I bucked and screamed, pulling on his hair and reveling in the ecstasy. The movement of his hand and the tenderness I still felt were a heady mix of pleasure and pain.

I never expected sex to feel this way. As I began to come down from my release, Hagen lifted me into his arms and carried me to his bedroom.

As he lowered me onto the bed and settled between

my legs, I said, "I thought you wanted me in the living room."

"Your first time should have been pure seduction and on a bed. Not in the office of a kink club. I want to remedy that."

Lifting up onto my elbows, I nipped his jaw. "I have no complaints. But if a bed is what you want, I have no objections."

"I'm happy you're willing to accommodate my needs." He turned his face and covered my mouth with his.

We savored each other until I couldn't stand the thought of not touching his bare skin. Pushing him back a fraction without breaking our kiss, I tugged at the buttons of his shirt

I wanted him as naked as I was. When my fingers wouldn't cooperate, I ripped his shirt open, sending buttons flying.

Hagen looked down at me and lifted a brow.

"You're not the only one who can make rags out of perfectly good clothing."

"Good to know." He bit my lower lip and then shrugged out of his torn shirt.

He slid off the bed and shucked his pants and boxer briefs.

Holy fuck. The man was built. Muscular yet lean. And those tattoos. There were two serpents designed with such detail that they almost looked three dimensional. They covered all of his right arm and up toward his neck, giving him the edge he was known for.

"What are you thinking about?"

"I want to explore your tattoos." I paused, licking my lips before saying, "With my tongue."

"Fuck, Starlight. You're going to kill me."

"So you'll let me?"

"Yes, but later." He climbed back on the bed—his cock hard and thick, bobbing up and down.

He grabbed a condom he'd thrown on the bed, tore the foil packet, and sheathed himself in latex.

"Much later. Right now, I need to fuck you the way I wanted to in my office." He grabbed my legs, spreading them as he pulled me toward him and impaled me on his erection.

"Hagen," I cried out.

"I love hearing my name on your lips." He pulled out to the tip and thrust back in.

He set a hard, fast, and relentless pace that had my body on fire and craving more. I dug my nails into his back and held on for the ride.

My hard nipples ached with the friction of his movement as did my core, wanting more and more. He cupped my jaw and drew me to him for a gentle kiss in sharp contrast to his thrusts. Then, before I realized it, I was convulsing around him. Milking his cock and soaking our bodies with my arousal.

"Come one more time," he murmured against my lips as his fingers brushed my clit. I followed his command almost immediately, but this time I wasn't alone.

Hagen

"I LEARNED you're a card shark today," I said as I tucked a well-satiated Persephone Kipos against my chest.

Watching her come apart in my arms was incredible. I would never get tired of seeing it. I planned to see it every day, if not multiple times a day. I should feel bad that I took her so hard. No matter what she said, she had to be sore, but the second I touched her, I lost all sense.

She lifted her head. "Is Zack still griping about the Rolex? It's not my fault he bet the damn thing and I had a royal flush."

I couldn't help but smile at her outrage. "I don't think Zack has met anyone better than him at cards. I believe you bruised his ego. He did, after all, finance his real-estate empire with his winnings from cards."

"Serves him right for telling me he'd go easy on me that first time he invited me to play."

"Who taught you?"

"Henna. You think I'm a shark. That girl is beyond that."

Starlight's cousin was smart as they came. Even with her own family issues, she'd gone out of her way to give Starlight a sense of family, and I'd forever be grateful for it. Too bad she had the bad sense to adore my father. But then again, Collin more than likely had ulterior motives for helping her after the scandal of her father's embezzlement.

"Maybe we should get Zack and her together for a game," I suggested but wasn't serious.

"Nope, never happening. First, the second Zack said anything against your father, she'd stab him in the throat. Despite what happened with the three of you, Collin has been more of a father to Henna and Anaya than my uncle ever was."

"And second?"

"I'm not sure Zack, with his master-of-everything-around ego, could handle losing to her. She is very much like him in personality." She shook her head. "They're both the winner-take-all type."

"In other words, you're saying they'd kill each other."

"You said it, not me. But yes." She shifted against my

reviving cock, and I had to set my hand on her hip to keep her still.

I will not fuck her again. I will not fuck her again.

Now if only my hard-as-stone cock was on board.

It would probably be months before I didn't get the urge to fuck her every second of every day. I knew it would be like this.

"I have something to tell you."

"Does it have to do with Papa?" Her body stiffened, and the relaxed mood dimmed.

"That conversation will happen with your brother present. But to ease your mind, I have a few people working on it."

I could tell she had more questions, but must have decided to let it go and instead asked, "So what do you need to tell me?"

"Pierce and Zack know you own PSK."

"Did you tell them?"

"No. It was Draco Jackson."

I waited for her to freak that a known monster was aware of her company, but she surprised me by staying calm.

"Well, that was unexpected. What did he want? A case of the batch I'm holding back from the market?"

I turned her to face me. "You know him?"

"I met him during my college years. His granddaughter, Lana, and I are friends."

"Do you realize how dangerous it is for you to be involved with anyone from his organization?"

"Calm down. She was my lab partner in college. I had no idea she was Draco's family. As far as I knew, she was a rich Japanese heiress who decided to become a chemist instead of going into the family business."

Family business being the mafia.

Draco had five children and fourteen grandchildren, with only one of them being a girl. She was the family princess. From what I knew about her, she was a science and technology wizard who'd attended Stanford. She rarely, if ever, gave anyone in her family grief. Well except that one time she went to... That was when it hit me.

"You were part of the group that went to Miami and had Draco losing his mind with worry."

She winced and then nodded.

"Yep. Imagine my surprise when a group of gun-carrying badasses walked into the nightclub we were partying at and ordered everyone but us to vacate the premises. At first, I thought we were in a hostage situation, but then a short Japanese man who looked exactly like Lana entered and glared at us.

"The crazy part was that he never raised his voice. Instead, he gave us a long lecture about responsibilities and showing respect, and we should know better than to cause our families undue stress. Afterwards, he kissed Lana on the head and told her she was a good girl."

I snorted—of course the old man let her get away with it. Too bad the poor chump bodyguard she ditched had to deal with the consequences of Draco's wrath. "When did you discover he was Draco Jackson?"

"It wasn't until midway through dinner in the penthouse of his hotel room, when he looked in my direction and mentioned you that I realized he was the mob boss you were reportedly working for. Lana's last name is Kimura, after all, so there was no way I could have suspected."

"What exactly did he say about me?"

Her cheeks heated and she looked away, which only made me more curious.

I cupped her jaw, turning her back to me.

"That he knew a good Greek boy I'd be perfect for once I finished school. He said the boy was headstrong but smart. Then he showed me a picture of you and told me we'd make beautiful babies. I think he views you as a son. Draco is really a nice guy."

"Those are two words I would never use when it came to describing *Oyabun*," I muttered.

I'd seen Draco slit a man's throat for talking without

permission. *Nice* was the last word I would think to use about him.

"So how does your whiskey come into play?"

"That was by accident. Lana knew from school that I was interested in the science behind distilleries. She's probably the smartest person I know. So naturally, I asked her to help me troubleshoot problems in my process in the beginning. She then helped me find my initial distributors. I'm not going to say I'm proud of it, but having Lana in the mix helps keep people from opening their mouths about who runs PSK."

All of the sudden, the urge to shake her hit me. My woman was in business with a mob princess.

"So you're in business with her?" I couldn't hide my irritation.

"Of course not. Lana is just a good friend. I help her when she needs help and she helped me. That's what friends do."

She couldn't be serious.

"I think you need to finish telling me the story, so I don't have a heart attack. How did Draco find out?"

"Honestly, I think he's always known. Lana is his pride and joy, and he knows everything about anyone and everyone in her life. Also, there's the fact he has been trying to sweet-talk me into giving him a case of the batch I'm keeping from the market. Lana let it slip a few months ago that she had a taste of the batch and that it was the best to date. Which of course means Draco wants some."

"Do you plan to give it to him?"

"Of course, but he'll have to wait until Christmas. Every December, I send him a case of my best bottling of the year. It's a tradition."

I stared at Starlight, not sure whether to be furious that she had a relationship with Draco or be in awe of her.

I rolled onto my back and covered my eyes. I'd spent so much time worrying about her being disgusted by my past, and here she was an almost granddaughter to a man tied to the mafia across two countries.

Starlight crawled on top of me, rolled her hips against my half-hard cock, and smiled. "Did I shock you?"

"You could say that." My hands gripped her hips, stilling her movement.

"I told you, I'm not as innocent as you think. Circumstances gave me the role I've played at Kipos, but I know what I'm doing. Well, when it comes to PSK, anyway."

I slid my fingers into her hair and drew her down for a kiss, then murmured against her lips, "Life with you is definitely going to be interesting."

"Hagen?" She whimpered, and the cords of my decision to not take her again began to unravel.

"Yes."

She shifted, lifting her leg as she grabbed the base of my shaft and pressed my cock into her slick opening.

Holy shit, that felt good. Her bare slick heat on my cock.

God, I wanted to bury myself deep in her.

Before I followed through with my urge, rational thought reared its ugly head, and I held her still. "Starlight. I'm not wearing a condom."

She gazed into my eyes. "You gave me your health report and you know I haven't been with anyone but you."

"But what about pregnancy?"

"I'm on the pill."

She laughed as she caught my frown and cupped my face. "My doctor put me on them to regulate my periods."

Why did the thought that she couldn't get pregnant if I came inside her bother me so much? This woman had me so twisted I didn't know which way was up.

In less than forty-eight hours, she had me tied in knots, and I wasn't sure how to handle it. I was the man every mother wanted to keep her sweet daughter away from, and here I was with the one girl I should never have touched.

"Please," she moaned as her arousal dripped onto my cock. "I need you in me."

Oh fuck, I was going to go to hell for sure.

I rolled her onto her back and slammed to the hilt. We

both gasped. The feel of her swollen, wet tissue had me gritting my teeth to maintain control.

Never had I gone without a condom. I wasn't the manwhore everyone believed by any means, but protections were something I lived religiously by. Hell, this was Vegas. But now, feeling the slick, wet heat of Starlight's pussy was like heaven on earth.

I set a steady rhythm, savoring her mewled moans of need and each slide off my dick in and out of her heat. Nothing had ever felt this good.

The first spasms of her release rippled around me, and I smiled as a thought passed through my mind. Time for her first lesson.

"Starlight, who do you belong to?"

Confusion entered her eyes as she clenched my shoulders and raised her hips to give her the friction she needed to go over.

I pulled out until I was barely a fraction inside her needy cunt and hovered.

"What are you doing?" she demanded, slapping my back. "I'm almost there."

I grabbed her wrists and pinned them above her head. "You have to answer my question, and then I'll give you what you're craving."

"Are you crazy?"

I slid my hand between our bodies and grazed the tiny

swollen pearl at the apex of her slit. I slowly pumped in and out of her while my fingers teased.

Her back bowed, and the tiny contractions started again. Just as she was about to go over, I stopped all movement. Then I repeated the pleasure-filled torture twice more.

"I swear to God, Hagen. I will kill you if you don't stop teasing me."

"It's not teasing. It's called orgasm denial."

She blew out a deep, frustrated breath. "I thought you said you weren't into kink."

"I never said that. I'm not into paddles and clamps and spankings. I'm into domination and control."

"Oh." Her green gaze dilated and her cunt grew wetter.

My cock ached to come, but I held back.

"Now answer my question."

"What question?"

"Who do you belong to?" I pressed my forehead against hers and stared.

A smile touched her lips, and she leaned up, grazing her soft cheek against my stubble-covered one before kissing my throat.

"Hagen, you know I belong to you. I wouldn't be here otherwise."

I cupped her jaw, covering her lips with mine. This woman never responded the way I expected.

As I deepened the kiss, I began to move, and within seconds, Starlight orgasmed, clenching hard around my girth. Immediately, I followed, and I could swear it never felt so good to come in my life.

It was settled. I was keeping this woman. Damn the consequences. She was mine. Hopefully, she wouldn't fight me on it when she learned what I'd decided.

CHAPTER TEN

Penny

"PENNY, I think you need to see this latest article about you."

I glanced over my shoulder at Anaya, who had a worried expression on her face.

It probably was some well-spun announcement about my departure from Kipos. Maybe something along the lines of having a mental breakdown and needing time to recuperate.

The fact that I'd spent the last three weeks out of sight and in Hagen's bed probably added to whatever Dara was leaking. A smile touched my lips. Being with Hagen was like being consumed by an avalanche of pleasure. When he wasn't working, he found some excuse to fuck me senseless.

It was odd not to go into the office every day, but it gave me some time to relax, catch up on work for PSK, and try my best not to nag Adrian for updates on all Dara was doing to destroy Kipos.

"Who cares?" I lifted my clipboard and wrote down a few numbers from the pressure gauge attached to the steel cylinders. "I was supposed to be here by six this morning. And since I haven't been here in two weeks and then overslept today, I have to catch up on too much to worry about my stepmother."

Anaya shifted on her feet and then sighed, walking over to a desk in the corner of the warehouse. She picked up a newspaper and brought it to me.

Begrudgingly, I took it from her fingers and scanned the contents. It was the business section of the paper. The headline read: "Greek Heiress Persephone Kipos Ousted from Kipos International."

The article underneath detailed my alleged involvement with the Vegas underworld and/or those with criminal ties.

It also relayed rumors of a torrid affair with one of the Lykaios brothers.

I bit the inside of my cheek so the ringing in my head would stop. I really hated that woman. I'd spent my whole life trying to keep out of the spotlight, and now Dara would try to ruin my reputation for what? To devalue the company? Kipos stock was going to take a plunge.

My stomach turned.

After a few deep breaths, I unbuttoned my lab coat and sat in a nearby chair. Pinching the bridge of my nose, I made a mental list of everyone I'd have to call to keep operations running.

Then, I remembered what Adrian had said.

Trust me. I've got it under control.

I wanted to let him take the lead on this, but he was only twenty. I hated allowing others to control my destiny, even my baby brother.

My CFO had recently heard that Dara was looking for a capital infusion into the company. She'd spent too much over the past few years, and the only way to keep a hostile takeover at bay was to sell equity shares of the company. Her best bet, though, was to sell the company outright. This way she'd have a hefty retirement, and Adrian and I would be done with her. Well, I would, but poor Adrian. She was his mother, and that would never change.

Too bad she needed my vote to go through with it. I owned thirty-three percent of the company, and the bylaws required my approval. If a bidder with enough capital surfaced, then I'd have to stall the vote until Hagen's contacts came through. I had to know for certain whether Dara was involved in Papa's death.

"The headline is bad, but if you read the whole article, they're saying this news goes against everything known about you. They think it's a ploy by your stepmother to ruin your reputation. Everyone knows she's after your..." Anaya trailed off when she noticed I was barely paying attention to her.

"Well, at least they got one part right." I closed my eyes, remembering the way it felt when Hagen slid inside me in the early hours of the morning.

Never would I have imagined a man could literally fuck all night, but Hagen had. My body ached, and my crazy self wanted more. It was a wonder I could walk today.

"What part?" Anaya came to sit across from me.

"The part about the affair with a Lykaios brother."

"Hagen," she said with a smirk.

My cheeks heated. "Yes."

"It's about damn time." She jumped up and fist-pumped in the air.

"I'm glad you're so excited about this."

"Whatever. I have no love life, so I have to live vicariously through you. Plus, you've had a thing for him since we were kids."

"You're still a kid."

She rolled her eyes. "Whatever. You know what I mean. So answer one question, and I'll leave you alone."

I crossed my arms over my body and waited.

"Is he as good in bed as the tabloids like to say?"

My blush deepened, and instead of answering her question, I said, "I think it's time we get back to work."

"Man, you're no fun." She did a pouty face that only a nineteen-year-old could get away with. "I bet if it was Henna or Amelia, you'd spill all the details."

I glared at her and tapped my clipboard.

"Fine." She threw up her hands. "Besides, Collin always said one day Hagen would get his head out of his ass and go after you."

I almost asked her to elaborate about that statement. As far as I knew, Collin was the last person to want anything good for Hagen. But I decided to keep quiet. I had way too much work to do.

For the next few hours, we worked tweaking the formula for the next distilling as well as the logistics of the bottling of the next barrels of the batch I liked to call the private reserve. I planned to hold it off the market for at least another year or two.

It was my best product yet, but it just wasn't ready by my standards.

If I was honest, I hated the marketing and distribution end of the business. My passion was the process, but I couldn't get one without the other. It wasn't until one of HPZ's subsidiary companies had contacted my public representative that I had considered selling the front-end part of the company while maintaining control of the back-end development and bottling.

Maybe in the future.

As of now, my focus had to remain Dara.

A beep sounded on the perimeter alarm, making me jump. Anaya was the first to glance at the surveillance feed. Her face got a bit of a dreamy quality as she saw Adrian's car.

Well, that was interesting.

I had mere seconds to linger on that thought before I saw Hagen pull up behind Adrian. He stepped out of the car and my heart all but stopped. He wore a fitted T-shirt and jeans, accented with a reflective pair of glasses that gave him a sexy edge.

"Well, hot damn, woman. That's who you're banging?" Anaya fanned herself. "Please tell me all of them are as hot as sin."

I stared at the monitor and felt the slow pulse of need Hagen's presence always ignited. "I guess. I don't view Pierce and Zack any different than I do Adrian. They're all my brothers."

"Let me be the first to inform you that Adrian is hot, so I bet Pierce and Zack are probably as smoking in person."

I scrunched my face. "You just made me nauseous."

The door to the warehouse opened, and Adrian, Hagen, and Zack walked in.

Zack? When had he gotten here?

Hagen had mentioned Zack knew about my involvement with Firewater, but I never expected him to come to the warehouse.

I glanced at the monitors again and saw his Porsche parked behind Hagen's. I'd been so focused on Hagen I never noticed the other car pull up.

"Hey, sis. Hey there, Ana." Adrian nodded to us and then moved to a bank of terminals he would tinker on whenever he was in the lab.

"Hello, ladies," Zack said, coming toward me and pulling me into a tight bear hug.

"Penny, I'm going to head out." Anaya checked her watch. "I'm supposed to meet Henna for a Krav Maga class in an hour. If I leave now, I'll have enough time to get home, change, and arrive at the gym before big sis can ream me for being late again."

I nodded. "Thanks for all the help today."

"You can pay me back with a cruise around the world when you make your first billion."

"Definitely." I smiled as I leaned into Zack.

As soon as the door closed, Zack asked, "How is my favorite underground bootlegger doing?"

I squeezed him tight and kissed his cheek. "It's not illegal, therefore no bootlegging."

"So what do you call this secretive production?"

I beamed up at him. "Incognito."

"A certain somebody told me it's called Firewater."

"No, that's the name of the reserve I'm working on. Firewater Incognito."

Anaya and I had only an hour earlier decided on the name of my special batch.

"Can I taste? It's the least you can do for taking millions from me over the last few years on your way to billionaire status."

"Not happening. And billionaire isn't a goal of mine, it's yours."

"How about a game—"

I cut him off. "I am not playing a game of cards for this."

He sighed. "It was worth a try. Then again, you'd probably swindle me out of my share of HPZ."

"Want to get your hands off her?" Hagen interrupted the banter and glared at Zack, who didn't seem to care and pulled me closer to him.

"Nope. We're fine right here."

It was apparent Zack was trying to get under Hagen's skin, but I wasn't willing to play that kind of game.

Not yet, anyway. Hagen and I were too new for

harmless flirtation. I slipped from Zack's hold and walked toward Hagen.

When I was a foot away from him, I paused. "Hi."

He watched me with the intensity I now understood as possessiveness.

Instead of responding, he cupped the back of my head and drew me toward him, kissing me mindless.

When he pulled back, he said, "You left before I woke up."

"Sorry," I whimpered.

My body was burning up and ready to jump him despite the fact I was sore.

Was I ever going to get enough of this man? We'd spent most of our time over the last few weeks fucking, sleeping, eating, talking, and fucking, and I wanted more.

Shit, I'd become a nymphomaniac.

It was the most hedonistic time I'd ever had. Hagen had essentially played hooky from his clubs to spend time with me, saying he paid people to keep things going when he was busy. I, on the other hand, had guilt for not being at Kipos but then had a sense of relief. It was as if, even for a few days, the weight of what happened to the company wasn't on my shoulders.

For all I knew, Dara had burned all my files and replaced me with a clown.

The thought had me smiling inside. All the sex I was having must have fried my brain.

"You could have left a note."

"Sorry," I repeated. "I was running late, and it slipped my mind."

I slid my palms up his forearms, loving the feel of his defined muscles, and lost myself in the intensity of his gaze.

"I don't like it when I have no clue what happened to you. Adrian tracked your car before I turned the city upside down looking for you."

"I had to work. I'm behind schedule. On a normal day, I'd get here by six and then head to the office for any early meetings."

"You don't have to worry about two jobs anymore. Set normal hours and focus on your distilleries."

A wave of sadness hit me for a moment before I pushed it back. No matter what I'd thought moments earlier, there was a sense of helplessness I couldn't shake. The future of Kipos International was out of my control, and if I was honest with myself, I'd never had any control to begin with.

The most important thing was to find out the truth about Papa's death and then devise a strategy to oust Dara. Selling the company was the last item on the list.

"From now on, if I'm still asleep when you're ready to

leave, wake me up." There was a determined fierceness to his words that had me studying him.

He was gorgeous as ever, but there was a hard set to his face.

Maybe this was part of being in a relationship, or perhaps it came with being in a relationship with Hagen.

He was way too serious. I was a nerd. How much trouble could I get into?

"Is there something you're not telling me? Am I in some danger or are you letting your possessive side go amok?" I leaned up on tiptoes, smirked, and gave him a quick kiss on the lips.

However, I noticed something pass in his eyes that made me think my joke hit the nail on the head.

"I want to go somewhere private."

"Umm." I glanced around. "Okay."

We were in an open warehouse. There weren't many places for privacy.

"We can go in the insulated lab." I pointed in the direction of my chem lab. "That is as alone as we can get here. Though the scent of all the fermenting barley may get to you."

"I have a better idea. Let's talk in my car."

"Adrian," I called.

"Yeah," he responded, lifting his head away from the monitors.

"Keep Zack entertained, and don't you dare let him mess with any of the machines. Zack has this need to touch things that aren't his."

"For Christ's sake, Persephone. I took your car out one time for a quick drive, and you act like I crashed it or something."

"You had the other poker players distract me so you could sneak out and get behind the wheel."

"You're too possessive of that car." A grin formed on Zack's face. "I have to admit, it was a sweet ride."

I rolled my eyes. "Don't touch." I pointed a warning finger at Zack and let Hagen lead me to the car.

"You are the only person I know who gets away with treating Zack like a dumb brother. If you don't know this, Zacharias Lykaios is probably one of the most ruthless businessmen around."

"Zack is Zack. The boy who'd tease me and pull my hair and get into mischief with me. I know without a doubt that if circumstances had been different for all of us, Zack and I would have been partners in crime giving our moms gray hairs."

Hagen remained quiet as if he was pondering my answer.

By the time I was seated inside his car, Hagen seemed to be in a brooding mood.

The second he closed the driver's side door he said,

"Why didn't you ever hook up with Zack? It's obvious that the two of you have chemistry. Hell, you have a history with Pierce too."

Wrinkling my nose, I frowned. "There are too many reasons to count why they do nothing for me."

"Name them."

"You're kidding, right?"

"You just said you and Zack would have been partners in crime."

Hagen gripped the steering wheel. Well, shit. He was seriously jealous of his brother. For such a confident man, he was really unsure of his appeal.

I released a sigh. "Hagen. They weren't you."

The fire in his eyes calmed.

"Come here."

I looked around. "What do you mean? In your lap?"

He nodded, pushing the button to move his chair back to the farthest point.

"But I'm wearing a skirt."

"I know."

"There are cameras everywhere. My brother does not need to see me straddling his boss's lap."

"Zack probably has him occupied with discussions of some new security software Adrian's developing for him."

Zack was notorious for finding some way to get the most work out of any given day.

"Fine." I climbed over the gearbox and positioned my legs on either side of his thighs as I held on to his shoulders. "Now what?"

His hands slid under my skirt, over my hips, and to the globes of my ass. He ground his hard length against the soaked slit of my underwear.

"Hagen," I gasped and then moaned as his thumb slid forward and grazed my clit.

"I want to fuck you right here. Right now. I want to tear the thing that you know you shouldn't be wearing and bury my cock so deep in your cunt that it permanently marks you. I want to fuck into you so hard that everyone and anyone knows you're mine."

I wanted that too.

"Yes. Anything, Hagen."

"But since I know you're sore from our early-morning antics, we'll have to settle for a bit of foreplay."

I couldn't help feeling disappointed. I wanted him to pummel my aching pussy, but he was right. I needed some recovery time. To go from never having sex to having it four to five times a day was going to take some getting used to.

"What does that mean?" I asked.

"It means I'm not going to fuck you, but I am going to make you so hot that you'll orgasm from my slightest touch."

"Okay."

"I want you to start by sliding your pretty pussy up and down the seam of my pants."

I followed his instructions, grazing my thong-covered slit over the stitching on his jeans. My sensitive clit ached as my core grew slick and swollen.

"Now. I want you to roll that cunt over my hard cock, showing me how you'd move if you were riding me."

I shifted my hips, grinding my damp heat against him and mimicking the slide of my pussy if there weren't any barriers between us.

All of a sudden, the familiar tingle I experienced every time I was with Hagen ignited, and my body took over. I rubbed and bore down on his hard and thick length until I shattered, bucking and screaming and coming so hard that I thought I was about to pass out.

"Hagen. Oh God, Hagen," I gasped, staring into his eyes.

"That was beautiful." Hagen's words were gruff and full of desire.

My face was flushed, my heartbeat erratic as I came slowly down.

Without thinking, I reached between us until my hand closed over his belt. Just as I pulled the leather through the loop, Hagen stilled me.

"What are you doing?"

I gave him a wicked grin. "Foreplay."

"I'm not going to fuck you."

"I know."

I freed his cock, sliding my hand up and down his hard, thick length.

"Starlight." He said my name as if it were a prayer. It sent a shiver down my spine.

I kissed him, taking his hands and using them to slide under my shirt to my breasts.

"I want to do something I read about in a book."

He pinched my nipples, and my core spasmed. "And that is?"

"Something similar to what we just did, but this time I want to get us both off with the slide of your cock between my pussy lips, with no barriers separating us."

For a split second I thought he'd say no, then he smirked. "Show me."

The fire in his blue eyes had nervousness creeping in. I had no idea what I was doing. It was obvious he'd just handed me the reins. God, I hoped what the romance novel said was accurate.

Pushing my thong to the side, I gripped Hagen's engorged cock again and positioned it against the lips of my sex. I rolled my hips to slide along his length, letting my slick arousal coat him.

The sensation was heady as he moved back and forth.

It was as if I had control but actually had .

the dazed bliss on Hagen's face, I could tell he'd .

this before either.

That thought brought a surge of confidence I had.
expected. He was the experienced one. The man with a
trail of lovers and conquests, and here I was giving him
something he'd never encountered.

The more I moved, the more the ache in my core grew.
Soon, my body took over as I increased the gyration against
him. I threw my head back, feeling my orgasm creep up. At
the same time, a low guttural sound escaped Hagen's lips.

"I'm close. Fuck. This is so hot. I'm not sure how long I
can hold out."

Hagen slid his thumb over my clit, and I detonated.
Ecstasy washed through my body. I bucked and ground
harder on his girth. My nails dug into his shoulders as I
rode out the pleasure.

The next thing I knew, Hagen lifted me and positioned
his cock at the entrance of my pussy and came, spurting
hot jets inside me. He held me over him until the last of his
release emptied out of him.

CHAPTER ELEVEN

Hagen

"WHAT NOW?" Starlight asked as she nuzzled against my neck.

"This was your plan, remember?" I reminded her.

This woman had rocked my world. Her innocence and desire to explore was throwing me for a loop. I was never into public sex. It was a hard-and-fast rule.

And here I was, coming in front of at least a dozen cameras and two people who probably wanted to kill us at the moment.

I was supposed to tell her about what I'd learned about the will. Instead, I was consumed by jealousy and a desire that I'd never experienced with any other woman.

"Hagen?" She lifted her head from my shoulder. "Why'd you come inside me? Were you marking me in some caveman fashion?"

"Yes," I honestly answered before I thought otherwise.

I wanted to mark every inch of her inside and out. I wanted every man within one hundred feet of her to know she was mine.

I wanted her forever. I wanted her round with my children. I wanted her... Fuck, what the hell was I thinking?

This woman made me feel too much and we'd barely begun.

I had to get control.

"And?"

"And what?" I said, hoping the coolness of my tone would get my mind back in order. "You're my woman. I can mark you with my cum wherever, whenever, and however I want." I closed my eyes and leaned my head back against the seat's headrest.

"Umm, okay." She slid off me and moved to the passenger seat. "You've put me in my place. I'm yours until you get me out of your system. Isn't that what you said the first time we were together?"

Immediately, I regretted my words, from a few weeks earlier and just now. I sounded like an asshole. She was more to me than she could ever know.

"Starlight."

She wouldn't look in my direction as she adjusted her clothes. There was hurt on her face and a sheen of tears in her beautiful green gaze.

"I'm sorry. I didn't mean it like that."

"It doesn't matter. Just tell me what you need to talk about so I can get back to work."

Her arms were crossed tight over her body, and her posture was ramrod straight.

"I'm sorry," I repeated.

"I said it doesn't matter. We will fuck as we agreed, you will help me prove Dara's involvement in Papa's death, and then you can move on to your next temporary conquest."

"Dammit. It's not like that between us. It never has been and never will be."

I was fucking this up royally.

"Could have fooled me." She turned her body away from me.

I set my hands on her hips and adjusted her back to face me, causing her to shove at me.

"Look at me, baby."

Releasing a resigned sigh, she said, "I'm not like your other women. I don't know the rules. I think it's better if we stop this before I get in too deep and end up hurt."

Before I could respond, she opened the car door and stepped out.

What the hell.

I jumped out and stalked past her, blocking her path back to the warehouse. She glared up at me and began to tap her foot.

"Get out of my way, Hagen. I don't care if you are over a foot taller than me, I will kick your ass."

This was probably not the time to tell her that I'd like to see her try.

"We are not stopping this. I fucked up. I was an asshole."

"Why?"

I hesitated, running a hand through my hair, and then decided to lay it out for her. "Because you make me feel things, want things. I have no idea how to handle it. My first instinct is to cut off my emotions. This is all new to me too."

"Oh" Her anger softened as did the stern set of her jaw. "So what are we? Yes, I know it's been only a few weeks since we got together but I have to wrap my mind around this."

I stepped toward her. "We are Starlight and Hagen."

"And that means what, exactly?"

"That we're a couple."

"For how long?"

Forever, I wanted to say, but that would more than

likely scare her shitless. So instead, I said, "Until you decide it's over."

She frowned. "I'm serious."

"So am I. If anyone does the breaking up, it'll be you. And for the record, this thing between us has been going on for over a decade. Getting in each other's pants was only the transitioning of our relationship into something more intimate."

She remained quiet, her face a play of emotions. She wanted to believe me, but she was still uncertain.

"Starlight, did you hear what I said?"

"I wish you would stop calling me that. I really hate my middle name."

"I know—that's why I like it. No one but me uses it."

She rolled her eyes as I slid my arm around her waist and pulled her toward me.

"Am I forgiven for being an idiot?"

"I suppose. I don't do well with hot and cold. I know I may seem a pushover, but I'm not. Especially with those who know me well. You're either in or out."

"I'm definitely in, but I can't guarantee I won't fuck up again. Being in a relationship is as new to me as it is to you."

"So this thing between us is a relationship? Does that mean we're exclusive?"

A crease formed between my brows. The thought of touching other women after having a taste of Starlight was repulsive. "Absolutely. When I said you were my woman, I meant it. Despite what the public believes, I have never had more than one lover at a time. Hell, I'm still friends with most of my exes."

"Okay. Good to know."

What did that mean? Maybe I shouldn't have brought up exes.

Never in my life had I felt like I had no idea what the fuck I was doing. It was like I was a teen again trying to figure out how to date a girl, not a thirty-two-year-old man with years of experience.

She remained quiet for a few more moments, and right as we reached the warehouse entrance she said, "Hagen, can I ask you a serious question?"

Well, that sounded ominous.

"Sure."

"Why do you play into the negative image about yourself? You're nothing like what everyone believes. Is it so bad if they see the decent, caring guy?"

I cupped her face. "The world sees what they want to see. I can't change it. Besides, my past played into my reputation. I've done most of the things people accuse me of. It's you who doesn't see the darkness in me."

"Or it's me that you show the real man behind the facade." She pulled open the door. "Since you and Zack crashed my secret lair, let me show you how

PSK operates and the bossy side of Persephone Kipos."

"Bossy? This I have to see."

Hagen

FOR THE NEXT HOUR, my mind was blown. Starlight was definitely bossy. Gone was the mousy pushover. She was a drill sergeant when it came to her business. If she asked a question, she wanted answers. If she wasn't pleased with a distribution deal, she expected a renegotiation.

For a moment, I'd thought her bottling manager was going to shit himself when Starlight had discovered he'd changed vendors for the bottles she preferred for Firewater. The fact she used science and the argument of flavor change against the use of, in her words, "subpar bottles," to justify the extra cost of the ones she liked was ingenious.

Even Zack was impressed to see this side of her. She ran a smaller empire than his, but it was beyond efficient.

She knew her business inside and out. It also explained her dual degrees in business and chemistry. It was apparent Kipos International was never her dream. The only reason she was fighting so hard to save it was Adrian.

He was the catalyst for everything Starlight did when it came to Kipos. She'd put up with Dara's oppressiveness and her manipulative antics instead of leaving town and never looking back.

She didn't need her father's company to survive. The fortune she'd inherited from her mother would keep her comfortable for the rest of her life. Not to mention what she'd received when her maternal grandfather had sold his Indian shipping empire.

The fact she had barely touched her fortune outside of taking some out to initially infuse into PSK Distilleries was remarkable. She could be like other wealthy heiresses—drinking, shopping, and being a complete waste of breath. She, however, chose to do something productive with her life.

As with everything, I'd kept tabs on her financial health. If the money wasn't tied up in trust after trust, I wouldn't have put it past Dara to spend every dime of it.

One day, I'd have to tell Starlight what I'd been doing. I only hoped she wouldn't freak. I was just trying to protect her, after all.

Who was I kidding, she was going to lose her shit.

"What are you thinking so hard about?" Starlight said

as she came out of her lab with her backpack over one shoulder.

"You have a remarkable operation. Not sure whether to be in awe that you had two full-time, energy-consuming jobs for the last few years or check to see if you're a robot."

She dropped her bag on the ground a foot from my feet and smiled up at me. "I believe, Mr. Lykaios, you've seen all my parts. Am I a woman or a robot?"

"Most definitely a woman." I gripped her waist and drew her to me, but stopped when Zack and Adrian walked in.

Adrian gave me an irritated glare and grabbed his own backpack. "Zack says the four of us need to talk. If you're done feeling up my sister, I suggest we head to Zack's penthouse at the Aegis. It's secure, and once we're done, I can review some work in the security office before heading back to the dorms."

Starlight pulled out of my hold. "Let me see what's eating him."

She threaded her arm in Adrian's, and they began an animated conversation.

Zack approached and shook his head.

"What?"

"Next time make sure the cameras aren't directly pointed at your car. Adrian went from raving about the new software he developed for you to wanting to kick your ass. No brother wants to see his sister grab a guy's hands and shove it up her shirt while straddling said guy."

"She was the one who climbed on top of me. I was only following orders." I couldn't help but grin.

"She isn't a short-term girl, Hagen. When it comes to her, what's your plan?"

My light mood disappeared and I clenched my teeth. I wanted to say it was none of his business, but he deserved an answer. Starlight meant something to him.

"I may not deserve someone like her, but I'm not sure I can ever let her go."

"And why don't you deserve her?"

"Are you kidding me? My hands are dirty. No matter how much I wish to sever ties with anything to do with Draco's business, I will always owe him. There is no getting clean from the past, and she needs a man without my baggage."

"Look. This is your life, but Penny doesn't seem the type to be scared away. I have a feeling she plans to keep you."

CHAPTER TWELVE

Penny

WE ARRIVED an hour later at Aegis, the largest of Zack's Vegas properties. I had only the time it took to get to the private elevators to take in the opulence of the hotel and casino. Where the Ida was clean lines with pops of color, the Aegis was richer in colors with dark shades, and the mood was decadence. This was the first mega property Zack had designed after he left the world of gambling and entered into land development.

"I'll meet you upstairs," Zack said. "Let me find Pierce. He should be in this conversation."

Hagen nodded, pushing the button to call the elevator. There was an uncomfortable silence in the air.

Hagen's hand brushed my lower back as I stepped into the cab, which garnered a frown from Adrian.

"What's wrong with you now? I thought we cleared things up at the warehouse." I glared at Adrian.

"Nothing." He folded his arms across his body and leaned against the wall.

"Obviously it is something and it has to do with me and Hagen. So, whatever you have left to say, get it out."

I'd thought the discussion Adrian and I had at the warehouse had resolved his issues with catching Hagen and me fooling around in his car. I understood that no one wanted to see their sibling making out with anyone. I'd apologized, but he looked like he still wasn't over it.

"Not now, Penny."

At that moment, the elevator jerked as Hagen pushed the stop button on the elevator panel.

"It's obvious you want to say something to me."

Adrian ran a frustrated hand through his hair. "Forget it."

His sullen expression made me realize no matter how mature he seemed, he was still so young. It had always been him and me against the world.

"No. You've got a problem with me, so let's hear it." Hagen leaned back against the opposite wall, pulling me against him. "We can sit in here all day."

"Fine. When I said give her a place to stay, I didn't expect you two to live together."

"It was her choice. I honestly had no say in it. In fact, I tried to convince her otherwise."

"Is that true?" Adrian turned his attention to me, adding, "I'll know if you're lying."

"He gave me the decision of having an apartment on a different floor or sharing his with him. I chose him." I crossed my arms in the same defensive stance Adrian had. "Plus, aren't you the one who told me to scratch my itch?"

Adrian's eyes grew big and his face reddened with embarrassment. "Penny, for God's sake."

Hagen lifted a brow in my direction, his lips curving at the sides and making my stomach flutter.

"Now—" Hagen's attention moved back to Adrian, "—tell me what the real issue is. As I said, we can wait in here all day."

"I get you're having sex, but seriously, she's my sister, man. I don't want to see you feeling her up."

I opened my mouth to reiterate it was my fault but Hagen squeezed my ass, telling me to stay quiet.

"Understood. We will keep it PG when in public. Anything else?"

"If you hurt her in any way, I will make sure the security infrastructure goes down at every company under HPZ holdings in a matter of seconds. I may not have the muscle, but I have the brains to fuck you up." The stern set of his jaw and the challenge in his gaze sent a pang to my heart.

"As I told your sister, she is the only one with the power to end us. As far as I'm concerned, she's keeping me."

I turned my face to look over my shoulder at Hagen. "Is that right?"

"Absolutely." His gaze was intense, sending butterflies into my stomach.

Adrian interrupted us by saying, "My concern is that you two are moving too fast. What has it been, like forty-eight hours?"

There was a hint of sarcasm in his tone that gave me the urge to smack him. I knew he was coming from a place of concern so I let it go.

"Three weeks. But by my count, this was years in the making." Hagen continued to stare at me. "We just let circumstances push us into action."

Before Adrian could respond, the elevator began to move, and Zack's voice came over the speaker. "Hey, assholes, move the discussion to the penthouse. Some of us need the elevator."

Penny

FIFTEEN MINUTES LATER, I was settled on a couch next to Adrian in Zack's palatial living room. He lived on the top two floors of Aegis. The living room, deck, and kitchen took up all of the bottom level. No matter where one stood there was a view of the Strip.

As with Hagen's place, the colors and decor were clean and simple. The place oozed wealth but in an understated fashion. This was a sharp contrast to the hotel under us, which was all about indulgence.

Hagen approached, handing me a glass of wine, and sat on the other side of me. "Zack, do you want to take this or me?"

"Go right ahead." Zack leaned against the marble bar near his kitchen and sipped his drink.

"Have either of you read your father's will? The one that was executed right before he passed?"

I frowned. "I have a copy of the will, and it was enacted a little after Adrian was born. There is no other will."

A look passed between Pierce and Hagen.

"Who gave you the copy you have?" Pierce opened a folder and set it on the table in front of Adrian and me.

"The family attorney, Trey Ritchman. He's worked for the family since before I was born." I never liked the man.

He'd always reminded me of a sleazy used-car salesman. Plus, after Dara came into the picture, he seemed way too attentive to her legal needs.

Would he have kept another copy of the will from us?

Yes, he would.

"Your father had a different firm draft this one. And we're positive Dara did not want you to know about it."

Adrian picked up the papers and began to read. His face grew a deep shade of red, and the vein on his forehead began to pulse.

"Adrian? What's wrong?" I touched his arm, but he didn't say anything for a few moments.

"If there was any doubt in my mind, there isn't now. She had Papa killed."

"What?" I tried to grab the papers from his hand, but he pulled them from my grasp and continued reading.

"Papa essentially cut her out of his will," he continued. "The only way for her to keep anything when I turn twenty-one is—"

"To sell Kipos." I finished his statement.

"How did you know?" Zack asked and came to sit in the recliner across from me.

"Because PSK's chief financial officer received an opportunity to bid on an equity share or buy out Kipos."

"Don't you dare do it, Penny," Adrian ordered. "I will

not let you spend your inheritance on a company neither of us wants."

I released a resigned sigh. "I won't lie. I thought about it, but even with my grandfather's money, I wouldn't have enough capital for the purchase."

"Why didn't you say anything sooner?"

"Adrian, I'm not sure if you realize this, but your sister's motivation for pretty much everything is you." Hagen ran his fingers up and down my back.

"Penny, I don't need you coddling me. I'm a grown man. If I have to work like the rest of the world, then I will."

"Dammit." My temper flared. "How do I go from watching out for you since you were a baby to letting go completely? Kipos is your inheritance."

"An inheritance I don't want," he countered, irritation radiating in waves from him. "Let her have the money. She'll spend it all within a matter of years, then she'll have to find some other way to fund her lifestyle."

"So you're fine with Dara winning? With her taking everything."

"No, I'm saying let her try to sell the shares. That was the plan from the beginning. The only way any sale goes through is if you agree to the purchase. According to the will, a direct blood heir of Kipos must sign and approve any major transition for the company. This includes mergers, equity sales, major contracts, and buyouts."

"That brings us to the next point of discussion," Hagen said, standing and moving to the bar for another drink. "You are now Dara's number-one target."

"And that means?"

Hagen hesitated to tell me. "Earlier today, *Oyabun* sent word that a few of his contacts are overly interested in you, which in his terms means that Dara has put a price on your head, if you don't agree to her plans for the company. Lucky for you and my sanity, Draco Jackson views you as a granddaughter and he put his own order out that if anyone touches you, he'll go after them."

I cocked my head to the side and studied him. "You're serious?"

Dara couldn't be that insane.

Who was I kidding? The woman had an end goal, and that was millions of dollars in her bank account. I was in her way, and she wouldn't think twice about getting me out of the picture.

"Yes," Zack answered. "But having Draco's protection doesn't mean you're safe."

"So what does that mean? Am I expected to walk around with security all day and night? If that's the answer, then I say not happening. I know about the shadow Hagen has on me. That should be enough."

Pierce shoved Hagen's shoulder as he came to stand next to him. "Told you she was smart. Your man isn't as good as you thought."

"Then I'll assign someone else. She has a habit of walking into potentially dangerous situations. I want her safe. If she isn't with one of us, she'll have our team with her at all times."

"I have a feeling she knows how to take care of herself." Pierce smirked in my direction.

"*She* is right here." I stalked over and glared at the two brothers. "She doesn't need your group of big, burly men to rescue her."

"Starlight, don't push me," Hagen warned. "You're my priority, and nothing will stop me from keeping you protected."

Ignoring him, I stabbed a finger into his chest. "Just so you know, whenever I traveled internationally for business, I've had a protection detail to ensure my safety. Do you honestly think I'd go into the jungles of Asia for a rare plant without security in place?"

He grabbed my hand and pressed it against his chest. The heat from his body was distracting.

"You can't be serious. Those women you have with you are as tiny as you. What the hell are they going to do? Stab them with their nail files and clock them with their designer handbags?"

"Um, Hagen." Adrian looked between him and me, releasing a sigh. "For your own good and at the risk of pissing my sister off further, I'd shut up."

"No, let him keep talking." I tried to jerk free of Hagen's hold, but he wouldn't budge. "Don't save this overgrown, chauvinist ass. Those women are members of some of the most elite agencies in the world. Their size means nothing. Every one of them could kick all your asses before you knew what hit you."

Then without warning, I used one of the moves I'd learned from Ameera, an agent in an underground human rights organization. I dropped, turned slightly, and threw Hagen away from me and onto the floor.

Utter silence filled the room.

"Want to tell me again that tiny women can't defend themselves?" I adjusted my disheveled shirt.

Hagen lay on the floor, staring at me as if I'd reared an ugly head. His face was flushed, and if I wasn't mistaken, he was aroused.

What the fuck? I'd just knocked him on his ass, and he was aroused?

I was never going to figure this man out.

The anger throbbing in my head was getting worse, and I knew if I didn't get myself under control, I'd get a migraine.

Zack leaned forward in his chair, smirking as Hagen

pushed himself to sitting. "Hagen, I'd stop while I was ahead. You're the one who said Penny isn't as naive as everyone believes. Maybe you should start listening to your own advice. Or I'm sure she'd be happy to drop-kick your ass into the next century."

CHAPTER THIRTEEN

Hagen

I WATCHED Starlight stomp out of the living room and onto the wraparound balcony. Never in my life had I been turned on by someone knocking me on my ass.

She wasn't weak, and I was an ass to believe she was, but that didn't mean I would go against my gut and let her handle it. We'd have to come to some comprise where both of us were comfortable.

"I suggest you fix this. The three of us are going to go downstairs to take care of some business," Zack said, gesturing to Adrian and Pierce.

With a frown, Adrian stood and then opened his

mouth to say something but stopped when Pierce spoke first.

"Let's go, kid. This isn't a conversation you need to be here for."

Releasing a frustrated breath, Adrian stalked toward the elevator.

I pushed up from the floor, hoping no one noticed the hard-on I was sporting, and waited for the elevator doors to close before following Starlight outside.

She leaned in the corner against the railing with her head resting on her arms as she gazed at the view.

"Starlight," I said cautiously.

She lifted her head and body. The anger radiating in her eyes almost had me stepping back.

"I'm not an idiot, Hagen."

"I know this."

"If that were true, then you wouldn't have believed I'd endanger myself without thinking twice about it."

"Wanting to protect you is a gut reaction. If I told you how long I've been trying to do that, you'd think I was stalking you."

Why the fuck did I confess that shit?

I walked up behind her. She stiffened for a second before relaxing as I slid my hand over her stomach and then gently pulled her against my front.

Her plump ass pressed against the hard ridge of my

cock, making me want to fuck her so hard that she'd agree to anything I asked in order to come. But that wasn't how I wanted her compliance.

I followed the direction she stared at and watched the bustle of the Strip below us. The daylight hours did nothing to dim the constant chaos of Vegas. But here with her, even with her anger, I felt I belonged.

"I already knew you were keeping an eye on me. The only way you would know about Firewater is if you had me followed. I figured this out after our almost-lunch."

"Almost-lunch?"

"We never got to lunch, remember?" Her cheeks flushed, and an image of her body bent over the railing while I fucked into her made my already straining cock ache for her as I'd never desired any other woman.

"I remember. We went straight to dessert."

"How does what happened constitute dessert?" She tilted her head and glanced at me over her shoulder.

"I had the pleasure of tasting your sweet lips and hearing the sound of your release. I've now gotten addicted to it. In fact, dessert should be the first thing on the menu whenever we're together."

She leaned into me, bringing with it a sense of relief. I buried my face in the delicate scent of her shampoo.

"Too many sweets are bad for you, Mr. Lykaios."

"I'm all about sinful pleasure."

The sound of sirens on Las Vegas Boulevard brought us back to reality, and the mood shifted.

"So what now?" She stared into the distance. "I won't go from one gilded cage to another. The fact you want to protect me doesn't make it any less stifling."

The last thing I wanted to do was keep her prisoner. Although, the fantasy of tying her to my bed in order to keep her safe was more than appealing.

"Dara is dangerous, and if she gets desperate enough, she will find other means to hurt you. I won't lose another woman I care about."

Mentioning my mother hit me like an arrow through the heart. I hadn't been there when Mama had gotten sick and barely had made it to her bedside to say goodbye before she passed away.

Outside of Mama, I'd never had any feelings for another woman. How was I going to convince Starlight to let my men watch over her when I couldn't? It wasn't as if I wanted any man but me near her at all.

"Look, I understand you're worried. If she had Papa killed, then she wouldn't hesitate to get rid of me. But I don't want to be smothered. I may not be part of Kipos, but I have a business to run."

"My goal isn't to smother you. My goal is to protect you."

If it were any other woman, I'd just order her to do what I said.

That was a lie. If it were any other woman, I'd have walked the second she became difficult.

Hell, it seemed like I was the one continually chasing her, wanting her to keep me like some lost fucking puppy.

"So what are you suggesting? I become your twenty-four-seven sidekick?"

"Or vice versa. I think I'd make a great lab assistant."

"Sure. I can see the great Hagen Lykaios taking instructions from me. I saw how you felt sorry for my plant manager when I laid into him for being late with his reports."

I turned her to face me and crowded her between my body and the railing. "No, I was turned on."

I pressed the length of my erection against the apex of her sex. She gripped my forearms, and a light flush crept into her skin, the first sign she was aroused.

"Make a decision. It's either me with you twenty-four-seven or one of my people."

She frowned. "How about one of *my* people? They've gone with me on every one of my international trips. Would that work?"

"Only if I've vetted them first." I wasn't going to let anyone watch Starlight's back without thoroughly checking their backgrounds.

"It's probably going to be more like they're going to have to vet *you*."

It was my turn to frown. "Meaning?"

"You're my first relationship. They'll want to make sure you're worthy of little old me."

I was definitely not, but I wasn't letting her go.

"So, you're saying they're like a group of overprotective sisters?"

"Something like that. On second thought, I'm almost positive they have every piece of information on you by now. They're very thorough when it comes to the people they protect."

"Who do they work for when not following you around the world?"

"Let me think." She tapped her chin. "Two are Masood, five of them work for British and American intelligence organizations, and two work for secret groups no one is supposed to know about."

"How the fuck did you find them? You don't just randomly meet a group of female intelligence agents looking to freelance as personal security."

"My best friend, Amelia. Her deceased husband had helped a few of them on a case, and they ended up friends. Now they watch out for her, her son, anyone Amelia wants them to protect."

"That doesn't explain how you met them."

"I was visiting her in Greece, and she'd been on my case about safety since I was planning to go to Indonesia to meet with a supplier of elderflowers."

I stared down at her. How long had she been gallivanting around the world? I'd only discovered her tendency to visit remote tropical places a few years ago. And what was this about a best friend in Greece? None of my investigations mentioned her. They said Starlight had a friend named Cara Thanos, a the widow of Stavros Thanos, a Greek entertainment mogul.

Then it hit me.

Why the fuck hadn't I thought about it? Amelia was Pierce's Amelia. She'd broken Pierce's heart and hadn't looked back. And when she'd married that Greek playboy, she started to go by Cara.

I'd interacted with Amelia on various occasions throughout my childhood. As the daughter of one of Collin's former gaming managers, she would attend parties and events put on by Collin. She and Starlight had gone to the same private school my brothers and I had attended. It had been years since I'd seen Amelia. Until now I hadn't realized she and Starlight had stayed in touch.

I reined in all the new questions I had for her, and instead, I said, "Go on."

"Amelia said she had a few friends who would keep me safe, and to ease her worry, I agreed to meet them." She shifted and then continued. "When I finally met the group, it turned out we all got along. After a while, whenever I traveled, I'd send them a message, and those who weren't on assignment would meet me for my trips. Most of the time when we go anywhere it isn't for my work, but just for a girl's trip."

"So in other words, you have an entourage of international agents to watch your back and to go on vacation with."

"You could say that."

"Now to another question that's plaguing me. How the hell have you been able to travel so much with Dara always keeping an eye on you?"

She beamed up at me. "I have a decoy."

"You have a what?"

"A decoy. My cousin, Mina, who lives in India, looks almost identical to me. Well, with the exception of the eyes. As far as Dara knows, I like to spend every vacation with my Mom's family in Greece. Mina is all for the cloak-and-dagger stuff. She actually loves it. For her, it's a break from her matchmaking family and tech job, and for me it's freedom."

It was like I had no idea who this woman was. Decoys, Mossad agents. What the fuck?

A headache began to brew.

Starlight cupped my face. "Am I freaking you out?"

"No."

"Liar."

I refused to admit that I wasn't sure what to make of her.

"As I told you, I'm not as innocent as you think. Yes, I'm not experienced in everything, but I have my own little secrets."

"Woman, you have more secrets than I do. I guess it means you trust me if you're telling me all this."

A crease formed between her brows. "Of course, I trust you. Did you think otherwise?"

Instead of answering her I asked, "Does Adrian know?"

"Yes. He's part of my cover with Dara."

"Last question, why didn't you use one of your ladies to help you find the answers to your father's death?"

"There are two reasons. One, they aren't allowed to do anything on US soil in an official capacity unless on assignment. And if I want anything to stick to Dara, it has to all be on the up-and-up. They can work as private security as long as they mobilize when their higher-ups call."

"And?"

"And two—" she hesitated for a second and then spoke, "—I needed an excuse to see you."

"But you wouldn't have seen me unless Adrian had arranged it."

"I was planning to get your help once Adrian gained his shares. He had other plans and moved up my timeline."

Her hand moved from my arms to the hem of my T-shirt and then under. The slightest touch was more arousing than having any other woman I'd ever fucked.

"So you planned to seduce me all along?"

She scored her nails up and down my back, making goosebumps prickle my flesh.

"Honestly I'd hoped it would be the other way around. Besides, I wouldn't know how to seduce you if I tried."

"You're doing an excellent job at this moment." Lifting her up by her legs, I wrapped her thighs around my waist, sliding her against my aching cock.

"Hagen," she gasped, digging her nails deep. "We aren't having sex on the balcony of your brother's house."

She arched against the friction I was creating between our bodies.

"Are you sure? We could always move it inside. There's a bedroom upstairs that belongs to me."

"We can't." Her hips gripped me tighter as she dropped her head to my shoulder. "I promised Adrian. I don't want to chance him coming up here."

"Fair point, Ms. Kipos. Adrian's a good kid, but I don't want to piss him off more than I already have."

I released her legs, letting them slide down my body until she was settled on her feet.

A moan escaped her lips, and I couldn't help but smile. "You're the one who said no sex."

"I know." She turned and braced her hands on the railing. "You're very potent, Mr. Lykaios."

"Feeling's mutual. Now that you've put a stop to the fun, let's get back to what started this discussion."

She released a sigh. "How about this? Until my friends get here, I'll let either you or one of your guys shadow me."

I smiled, feeling a sense of victory.

"But the second you become overbearing it ends."

"I'm never overbearing."

"Tell that to Pierce and Zack. They told me that you had Draco's men watching them all through college so they wouldn't get in trouble. Zack said you were a cock block."

"My brothers need to shut their mouths during your poker games."

"Hey, getting them to chat is the best distraction. How do you think I win?"

"From what Zack says, you can read people, and then you let them double or triple the pot before you nail their heads to the table with whatever you were hiding."

"I'll never admit to anything."

"Want to try your hand at the tables of Ida? I hear the owner has a thing for secret chemists with emerald eyes."

"Why not? I've taken more than enough money from Zack over the years. Let's see if my luck holds."

CHAPTER FOURTEEN

Penny

"WOW. Hagen is going to go nuts when he sees you," were the first words Pierce said as I came out of Hagen's private elevator.

I glanced down at the one-shoulder sequined minidress Henna had sent over and made a mental note to thank her. If there was one thing she knew as well as the hotel business, it was fashion.

The style flattered my petite frame, and with my hair and makeup done just right, I felt sexy.

The last time I'd dressed up like this was when Amelia had taken me to Ibiza for a night out on the Spanish island.

It had been for her birthday a few months before her husband passed away.

"Thank you." I slid my arm through Pierce's elbow. "You don't look too shabby yourself."

The Lykaios brothers were definitely blessed with devastating good looks. Pierce was the most athletically built of the three with a physique that was a cross between a lean swimmer and a prizefighter.

"Why, thank you. I thought it was fitting to dress up for the owner of everyone's favorite spirit."

From a distance, I noticed two men with earpieces watching us.

"Where's Hagen?"

"He had to handle an issue. He told me to take you to the private poker players' lounge."

"Should I be honored that I'm about to take on some of Vegas's biggest whales?"

Pierce smirked. "You're the whale in that room."

"We'll see."

As we walked through the main casino, I couldn't help but want to join the enthusiasm of the various people crowded around the tables.

"No."

I glanced at Pierce. "What?"

"I have strict orders to take you upstairs."

I gave him my version of puppy-dog eyes that would get me my way when I was younger. "Please."

He groaned and shook his head. "Hagen is going to kill me."

I squeezed, leaned up, and kissed him on the cheek. I grabbed his hand and dragged him toward a blackjack table.

Just as I was about to reach into my purse to pull out my card to buy in, Pierce handed me a card. "At least this way, when you win, it nets even. We can't lose money if it already belongs to the casino."

Pulling the card from his fingers, I inserted it at the table and bought five thousand in chips.

"That's a hefty advance."

"I know the owners. They won't mind."

For the next twenty minutes, we played various games around the casino. I won a lot more than I lost and was about ten thousand ahead.

"Pierce, can I ask you something?"

"The way you phrased that, I feel like I'm in trouble."

"No. It's nothing like that. It's just a question I've wondered about for years."

"Go ahead."

"Are you still in love with Amelia?"

His expression darkened. "That was over years ago. She married another man."

"I know. I just wonder sometimes. You never date anyone seriously."

"Don't try to play matchmaker. I know you two are thick as thieves, but she's my past."

"Fine. I'll drop it. Just know not everything was as it seemed at the time."

Pierce sighed and kissed my forehead. "Thanks for not picking sides when everything went down."

"You're both my family." I glanced to another area of the room and found a way to change the subject. "Roulette, come on."

We found a spot along the table and waited for the other places to fill.

"Place your bets," the dealer called.

I set all my chips on black thirteen and grinned at Pierce.

"Figures you'd put all your eggs in one basket. Do you ever pick any other number to start?"

"Nope. It's lucky."

"It wouldn't have to do anything with the black sheep of the family whose favorite number is thirteen."

"Perhaps."

"No more bets." The dealer dropped the ball onto the roulette wheel.

I focused on the ball spin and then looked up to find Hagen watching me.

My heartbeat accelerated. It should be illegal to look so good. Hagen wore a black-on-black custom-fitted suit that did nothing to disguise the honed body hiding underneath.

He sipped a familiar red liquor with one large round ice cube.

His eyes blazed with lust. I licked my lips, feeling my cleft swell and grow damp.

"Black thirteen," the dealer called.

Hagen lifted his brow when he saw the dealer push my winnings in my direction.

I shrugged my shoulders and mouthed, "Beginner's luck."

He set his glass on the tray of a nearby server and stalked toward me.

"I see big brother is here, and now I'm chopped liver."

Hagen stopped a bare foot from me and then said over my shoulder, "Get lost. Your services are no longer needed."

I turned toward Pierce. "Thanks for showing me around."

"See you later, shorty." Pierce kissed my cheek.

When I looked back at Hagen, he was frowning.

"What?"

His hand gripped my waist. "You're mine."

"Yes."

Hagen gestured to a man standing in the corner. In the next minute, he was gathering my chips.

"Your winnings will be delivered to the lounge."

"Are we going somewhere?"

"Yes. I learned you have a thing for pastries. Let's go have dessert." His lips quirked up at the corners, and I knew his mind went to his version of dessert we'd engaged in not so long ago.

"Damian told you."

Instead of answering, he held out his hand. I slid mine over his and let him lead me to the patisserie. As we neared, a well-dressed woman in a chef's coat and hat approached.

"Mr. Lykaios, we have a table ready for you. I hope you enjoy." She smiled as we passed her and moved in the direction of our table.

"Is that..."

"Yes." He answered before I finished my question. "This is her patisserie, after all."

I was obsessed with Micola Trudeau and her unique cooking style. She had a French and Greek background that created a taste that was not exclusively Greek or French but a combination of both.

"I am so going to beg her for cooking lessons before I leave."

He paused midstep and faced me. "Are you planning on going somewhere?"

"Well, I wasn't sure if you were serious about me staying long term."

Shit, why'd I confess that?

"Starlight, as I said, the only way this ends is if you end it."

"That's a lot of power you're giving me."

"I know." He kissed my forehead. "Time for dessert before you meet your opponents."

"You make them sound like I'm about to go against a band of mercenaries."

"Close. The men and women you'll meet tonight are the best in their fields. So, needless to say, they play poker the way they do business."

"So do I."

"That is why I knew you'd fit in."

We took our seats, flirted, and made small talk while we ate. It was as if we were on a date, and I loved it.

Just as a server refilled my coffee, Hagen said, "I want you to know as much as possible about the people you're playing with. They will have researched you and won't hesitate to use any advantage."

"Okay. That's to be expected." I lifted my cup, taking a sip. "Tell me the deets."

Hagen set his saucer down and leaned back. "Hector

Cortez runs all the fruit and potato exports out of Peru. He has an ancient mindset about women and their place in the world."

"I'll try not to stab him with the heel of my shoe if he pisses me off." I smiled up at him, and he shook his head.

"Jason Sev," Hagen continued, not hiding his amusement at my statement, "is a Norwegian aristocrat. He likes to party and lives the typical wealthy European jet-setter lifestyle.

"Kacee Hightower is a Texas billionaire. He's rough, tells it like it is, but is the kind of man you want to have your back. Out of all the players, he's the one I think you'll like the best.

"Navin and Ming Seif are twins who do nothing without the other. They are tech industrialists. They rarely, if ever, talk, but will think nothing about betting a few million dollars if there is even a remote chance of winning the hand.

"The last player is Briana Amici. I think you two will get along. She is the heiress to an olive oil fortune. She could fill her days traveling and engrossed in fashion but prefers to spend her time in the olive fields."

"So what did you tell them about me?" I asked after I swallowed the last bite of my pastry.

"That you're gorgeous beyond belief, have brains to

match the beauty, and can drop-kick a man if he pisses you off enough."

"I'm serious."

"They know you are the Kipos heiress and my girlfriend."

"So in other words, they think the only reason I'm at the table with them is because I'm sleeping with you?"

"They all will know you're smart with your degrees. But they will assume it was nepotism that got you your position at Kipos and made you successful. It's your job to let them underestimate how intelligent you truly are. Isn't that what you've mastered over the years?"

"I guess." I frowned. "With Dara, I had no choice."

"Think of tonight like you did that first game with Tweedledum and Tweedledee."

"I'm not sure Pierce and Zack would approve of your description of them." I paused. "Am I your girlfriend?"

"You're more than that, but for now, we'll call you my girlfriend."

"Then what are you to me?"

A sheepish grin crossed his face. "Your master of sin. After all, you did task me with the corruption of Persephone."

Penny

TWENTY MINUTES LATER, after brief introductions, I slipped into my seat at the poker table. All the seats were occupied except one. The people around me were studying me and each other. I'd learned that none of them had played together before, with the exception of the twins.

The dealer glanced at Hagen, who looked at his watch and gestured to wait.

A few moments later, a leggy blonde with a bombshell figure strolled in.

"Sorry, darlings. I was held up," she said in a heavy Italian accent. She wore a cat-like bodysuit with thigh-high boots. She had the dominatrix look down pat. The only thing missing was a whip.

A bubble of excitement filled me, and I nearly jumped out of my seat and ran to hug her. The first of my girls had arrived, and in the form of the Italian heiress she actually was.

"So, who are you?" Sauntering in my direction, she examined my outfit from my shoes to my head and hummed. "I like the dress."

Hagen shifted to stand behind me. "Briana Amici, this is Persephone Kipos."

She shook my hand, and I felt her slip something into my palm. I knew what it was—a tracker in the form of a ring.

"It's nice to meet you. I love your family's olive oils. They're a staple in my house."

"It's good to see someone who appreciates quality over the crap they sell in the supermarkets."

She took her seat across from me and picked up the cocktail an attendant set in front of her.

Dropping my hands into my lap, I slipped the tracker onto my right ring finger.

Hagen noticed the movement and leaned over to whisper, "I take it that you know her."

"Yes."

Then he added, "Please tell me she isn't one of your entourage."

"Yes, she is. She's usually the team leader."

He brushed his lip against the side of my neck, sending shivers up my spine. "Only you would have the most temperamental diva around as part of your security detail."

"It's an act." I leaned into his touch.

"As I said before, you're full of secrets."

"Let's begin," Ming, one of the twins, said.

Hagen stepped back and nodded to the dealer to start.

For the next two hours, we played. I lost the first few rounds, studying the group and gauging the little nuances that gave away their thought processes. I was pretty sure Hagen was scratching his head and wondering how I beat his brothers.

"Call," the dealer said, expecting everyone around the table to add to the pot or bow out.

The twins and Jason folded, leaving me and three others in the game.

"You sure you don't want to fold, missy? Maybe you'd be better off playing the slots downstairs." Hector gave me a condescending smile.

Hagen's warning about Hector's stance on women was more than obvious. The man couldn't go one round without making some underhanded comment.

"No. I'm where I'm supposed to be."

"Leave the girl alone." Briana glared at Hector. "We're tired of your chauvinistic anecdotes."

Hector ignored her and leaned back to look over to where Hagen watched the game from a set of sofas in the corner.

"Your girl is pretty to look at, and I'm sure she's fabulous in bed, but I wouldn't mistake her for a high roller."

A tic pulsed in the side of Hagen's head, telling me he was about to knock Hector into the next century.

"Sometimes first impressions can be deceiving." Hagen glanced in my direction and gave me a wicked grin that shot straight to my core. "The most dangerous opponents come in packages mistaken for harmless."

"I bet this one has nothing better than a pair. Let's see them."

I held in my sneer and couldn't wait to see the asshole's face.

Laying down my cards, I gave no reaction but to lean back and pick up my drink.

"Ha-ha." Briana clapped her hands. "Hector, I hope you have something to beat a straight flush."

"What?" He stared down at his cards. "How the hell?"

"It looks like our little wallflower here is a killer waiting in the wings." Kacee lifted his tumbler and clinked his glass against mine. "I can tell this game is about to get interesting."

We played for another hour and a half. The twins, Jason, and Hector withdrew from the game when Hagen announced the thirty-minute mark until the end of the play.

"Fold," Kacee said as he dropped his cards to the table and shook his head. "That's five hands in a row. Tell me you had something better than two pairs."

"Of course she doesn't, darling," Briana purred while stirring the olive in her martini. "Isn't that right?"

I gave them a sheepish grin and revealed cards that would have lost the pot had Kacee stayed in the game.

"You had nothing. Damn girl, you have the best bluff I've encountered in years. Those sweet smiles are what gets a man, and then before anyone knows it, he's lost over a hundred grand." Kacee picked up his cigar, gave it a few puffs, and set it down on the ashtray. "I need you to come work for me."

"She doesn't need your money. She has a fortune of her own." Briana smirked. "Plus, a very possessive nightclub owner would be very upset if she went to work for the competition."

Kacee looked at Hagen. "You better put a ring on her finger, or I'm going to steal her."

I flushed. That was not something either of us had thought about or discussed. Hell, we'd been a couple for barely three weeks.

"I'm working on it."

What?

I whirled around in my seat and locked eyes with Hagen. There was a hint of humor in his gaze but also a touch of truth.

He couldn't be serious. Could he?

He lifted a brow in challenge.

My heartbeat pounded into my ears as did a longing to truly belong to him. For years, it had only been Adrian and me. My role was to protect him and do my damnedest to raise him while growing up myself. But in all that time, I never felt there was anyone who was mine.

Hagen implying he wanted a future with me made me nervous that I was getting carried away.

Before I could react, a group of men entered the lounge followed by a few of Hagen's security and two pissed-off Lykaios brothers.

"We've come to join the party."

CHAPTER FIFTEEN

Penny

THE AIR in the room grew cold, and the casual mood disappeared.

It was apparent the group wasn't welcome.

Hagen looked toward Zack. "Why are they here? I thought we had an agreement."

The men began to order drinks from the hostesses. Their accents sounded Eastern European, but which country I couldn't place.

"They decided to make an unexpected U-turn. I think you may need to have a nice chat with their boss. I really don't want any more energy expended to deal with their bullshit."

"Deal us in," said a tall man in the back as he looked everyone up and down before his attention focused on me. There was a hint of surprise and then a calculating grin.

Oh shit, that was the guy in Dara's office the day she fired me. Now that I thought about it, I'd seen him multiple times over the years—at her office, her penthouse, and on trips with her.

What was his name? *Erin Kapok.*

I remembered Adrian mentioning some Ukrainian lover Dara had an on-and-off thing with for the last few years. According to Adrian, he worked for a European mob syndicate.

Trust Dara to fuck a mobster to get her dirty work done.

"Hagen, that's one of Dara's lovers," I whispered.

He moved closer to me and said in a low voice, "Now this is starting to make sense. Whatever he says, do not respond."

I wanted to argue but kept quiet as Kapok stared me down. He knew I recognized him.

A few more of Kapok's men entered the room but stayed back, remaining close to the door, watching and trying to understand what was happening. They spoke in what I could only assume was Ukrainian. They all seemed irritated with Kapok but moved to the side to watch.

"Sorry, Kapok, the game is over. We're about to have

dinner," Zack said as Hagen moved to stand between Erin and me, blocking his view of me. "The lounge next door has room for a few more to join if you're bent on playing."

"What's the buy-in?" Kapok asked, shifting to my line of sight again.

"Two hundred thousand. The same as always. If you follow Jamie, she'll get you settled next door." Zack's voice was cold, and with the unquestionable authority he was known publicly for.

Kapok began to move but paused. "I have a question."

Everyone waited. I knew whatever he said would be an insult directed at me. He was too focused on me, and Hagen's protective gesture toward me gave away I was important to him.

"Did the Lykaios whore have the buy-in or was it paid by being on her back? According to her stepmother, she's fucking all three of you."

The room grew quiet.

Briana jumped to her feet, and I cringed, thinking she was about to pull out her gun and shoot him. Instead, she exclaimed, "*Stronzo.*"

"Now see here, boy. She is a lady, and you will respect her." Kacee rose from his seat, but stopped when Hagen lunged toward Kapok.

"You son of a bitch. Don't you ever call her that."

I quickly grabbed Hagen's arm and stood, moving in

front of him before he lifted his clenched fist and punched Kapok.

Hagen tried to shove me behind him again, but I wouldn't budge.

This was the exact reaction Kapok wanted. There was a smug satisfaction on his face. I'd seen that same look on Dara the countless times I'd listened to her insult me.

I was not going to let the bastard get away with degrading me. If he wanted to believe I fucked all of them, fine—who gave a shit?

At that moment, extra security rushed in and glanced at Zack, who nodded toward Kapok.

"Get rid of him. He is no longer allowed on any of our properties."

"Get your hands off of me." He struggled against their hold. "Admit it. Dara was right."

"Fine. If that's what you want to believe. I'm the Lykaios whore. It's better to be their whore than Dara's."

"Starlight." Hagen's eyes were filled with rage. "I told you to stay quiet."

"I was only—"

He cut me off. "Go with Pierce while Zack and I take care of this trash."

"He's not worth it, Hagen."

"Pierce. Get her out of here." Hagen's voice was ice like I'd never heard before.

Zack spoke next. "Ladies and gentlemen, if you wouldn't mind vacating the room, we have a reception waiting for you."

Pierce pulled me from the room as it emptied.

"This is my fight. Dammit, Pierce."

"No, it's his. Hagen is an enforcer. It doesn't stop just because he doesn't work directly for Draco anymore."

"What's that supposed to mean?" I jerked my hand free to enter the elevator.

"Being with Hagen means dealing with the darker side of what he does. He isn't the Prince Charming you've conjured in your mind. He's lethal and won't hesitate to get his hands dirty. Especially when someone who knows better insults his woman."

"You make it sound like I'm some kind of liability." I folded my arms across my body as we entered the elevator.

"That is what you are. You are his weakness. Hagen has a reputation for staying calm in almost any situation. The fact he had any reaction when Kapok insulted you means you're his weakness. People like Kapok's boss won't hesitate to use that information. If Hagen doesn't take care of it, then it will put you in danger far bigger than your issues with Dara."

"So you're telling me that Hagen is going to make it clear that if anyone messes with me, they mess with him?"

"Exactly."

"That's seriously archaic."

"That's life with Hagen. You are his, and therefore people will use you against him. Just know Hagen will kill anyone who tries to hurt you. That includes using the tools he learned at Draco's right hand." He saw me cringe. "He loves you, Penny—he always has. You need to decide if you can deal with it or not. If you can't handle it, break it off now."

CHAPTER SIXTEEN

Penny

"TAKE ANOTHER SHOT. It'll help calm you down,"
Henna, my cousin, said to me as she set the third tequila
shot in front of me.

We sat on the terrace bar of one of the outdoor
restaurants at Ida. The cool breeze of the evening should
have felt refreshing, but all it did was irritate me since I
was sitting outside while the men took care of business.

"Aren't you the enemy? Why would Zack call you
here? You work for his father."

Henna tied her long black hair into a ponytail and
leaned forward with a grin. "Because you have two of the
Lykaios brothers scared shitless. I don't think any of them

have seen you so pissed off. And it wasn't Zack who called. It was Pierce."

I thought about it and sighed.

"I know you better than most people and you're about to go into silent treatment mode. Which means you will brood and get madder and madder until you boil over and explode on Hagen."

"Whatever," I muttered. "He'd deserve it."

She shook her head and grinned at me. "You're so cute when you're angry. Come on. Take another shot with me. It might cool your temper."

She clinked her glass against mine and we did the standard lick, slam, suck of a tequila shot.

I let the fiery liquid burn down my throat. Immediately, with a gesture from Henna, another shot appeared.

"I think you're trying to get me drunk."

"No, I'm trying to get you to chill out before you head up to your penthouse in the sky and the man waiting for you. By the way, Pierce thinks you're going to retaliate by jacking up the price on your alcohol."

"It was a thought," I answered her statement. "But Hagen was right. I should have kept my mouth shut."

When Pierce had pulled me from the lounge, I was ready to fight. I was enraged that they would try to keep me from standing up for myself.

Then when he implied I was Hagen's weakness, my anger had disappeared.

I was still pissed that Hagen would have to deal with Kapok and send a message to his boss, but I wasn't mad at any of the brothers.

The role Hagen had played as Draco's enforcer wasn't something he'd chosen but had been selected for him. From the beginning, I'd accepted that there were aspects of his life that weren't comfortable or accepted by the public at large.

I knew he never wanted me to see the darker side of his life. And because I'd let my temper get the best of me, he'd had no choice but to show me.

"What to elaborate?" Henna asked.

Briana slid onto the stool next to me. "Let me do the honors. She called herself the Lykaios whore and nearly made Hagen's head explode."

"It was definitely not one of my better moments." I closed my eyes and lifted my face to the sky for a few seconds. "My only excuse was that I was sick and tired of others thinking I'm helpless and letting people dictate my life. So, I decided to stand up for myself."

"Yeah, against a man tied to a Ukrainian mobster. That isn't someone you handle alone, no matter what your pride tells you."

"Wait. You left that part out." Henna and Briana

shared a look. "Didn't you learn anything from the incident with that douchebag in Indonesia?"

"Apparently not," Briana muttered. "I came here to help protect your ass, and that means following the rules we set up. One of the most important being 'do not antagonize mobsters.'"

"I swear, Penny. You are so hard-headed." Henna glared at me. "Bri and the girls can only do so much. With Dara wanting you out of the picture, you have to be smart and not let emotions get in the way."

I pressed my fingers to my eyes. They were right. I'd wanted so much to stand up for myself that I didn't think that having Hagen handle the situation would have been smarter and safer.

"I guess I owe all three of the guys an apology."

"For Pierce and Zack, yes." Briana gave me a calculating grin. "For Hagen, a nice blowjob should do the trick."

Henna snorted. "I concur. Get your ass to your apartment and grovel. Hagen may have a reputation as a badass, but he will easily forgive you if you make it worth his while."

"You two are incorrigible."

Penny

I ENTERED Hagen's penthouse ten minutes after leaving Briana and Henna to their cocktails. The second the doors opened, the exhaustion of the day weighed down heavily on my shoulders. All I wanted, besides the man who'd turned my world upside down, was an extra-large helping of wine and a soak in the hot tub.

First, I'd have to do some groveling as the girls suggested.

"Hagen," I called, "are you home?"

Silence.

"Well, shit." I slipped off my shoes and dropped my clutch on the table by the door.

I looked out at the lights of Las Vegas and shook my head. It was still unfathomable that I now lived on the Strip with a man so many referred to as the god of the underworld. If only people knew he wasn't the bogeyman everyone believed him to be. Well, not to me, anyway.

A shudder went through me as I remembered the rage in Hagen's eyes when Kapok had referred to me as the Lykaios whore. Then shock when I'd said the same thing.

Thankfully, Pierce had gotten me out of there before I let my emotions go further. Now I'd have to face the wrath of Hagen once he finished up for the day.

I'd better enjoy the short respite I had.

I walked toward the balcony, opened the door, and stepped into the warm summer breeze. The pool reflected the night sky and made me think of how surprisingly quiet it was up here—a complete escape from the hustle and bustle of Sin City below.

Grabbing the remote for the hot tub, I set it to a toasty one hundred and two degrees. Maybe after I soaked my tired muscles, I'd take a cooling dip in the pool.

Just as I replaced the remote in its holder, I noticed a shadowed figure sitting in a corner. For a split second fear hit me, then I recognized the build of the man and the tumbler in his hand.

"Hagen?"

"So you're my whore?"

"I..." I wasn't sure how I was supposed to respond. "It's what some people believe."

"What do you believe?"

I released a breath. How to answer his question?

"I'm not a whore. But I have no problem being your whore." I paused and then added, "As long as I'm the only one."

He sat up, setting his drink on a table next to him. The light hit his sapphire gaze, revealing a hunger that had me wanting to take a step back.

"Is that so?" His voice grew a bit gravelly, tinged with his arousal.

"Yes."

A wicked smiled touched his lips and my sex clenched.

"Then come here and show me."

I hesitated for a flash of a second before I slowly moved toward him. When I was barely a foot from him, he set his hand on my hips. His fingers branded the outside of my thigh. My palms settled on his shoulders, and I stared down at him.

Hagen held my gaze as he tugged up my skirt and then slid his thumbs under the material. He grasped the thin straps of my thong, pushing the silk down. "Step out of them."

I followed his order and then waited. His focus moved to my wet sex. He licked his lips.

God, I wanted his mouth on me. But I knew it wouldn't be so easy. He was still pissed from earlier, and I had no doubt he planned to make it very hard for me to calm him.

What he couldn't understand was that I'd rather be his whore than another man's lover. He brought out a side of me that I never believed I could explore. He thought he was corrupting me, but in fact he was freeing me.

"Now I want you to take off your clothes, leave on the bra. Then go sit on the edge of the hot tub."

I watched him, not sure what he was planning.

"I gave you instructions, Starlight."

I snapped out of my thoughts, removed my dress, and moved to the travertine surround of the hot tub.

Sitting down gently, I waited to see what Hagen would do next.

He slowly stood, revealing a small gift bag in his hand. I took it from him, not sure whether to look inside or wait.

"Take it out," he said before returning to his seat.

I stuck my hand in the bag and wrapped my fingers around a small, rubbery object. The feel of it told me what it was before I saw it.

"A vibrator?" I questioned, pulling it out.

It was black, small, designed with a curve to fit into a woman's palm.

"Yes. It's called a Lily. Thought it was fitting since I'm the man who deflowered you. Might as well continue the plucking."

I swallowed. "You want me to use it here?"

I glanced around the open space and then back at him. I wasn't new to masturbation, but it was something I'd done in private, with no one around, with toys I'd bought for myself.

"Yes. I want to see how you get yourself off while you're fantasizing about me."

It was almost on my tongue to ask him why he would

assume I was thinking of him as I came, but a lift of his brows told me he knew I'd be lying if I denied it.

I licked my lips. "I'm not sure I can do this with someone watching."

"I'm not just someone. Besides, I'm not giving you a choice." He sat back, picking up his tumbler. "You wanted me to corrupt you. That is what I'm doing. Now spread those legs and let me see you pleasure the pussy that belongs to me."

Biting my lip, I pressed the button to start the vibration of the device.

"Set it to medium. I don't want it to be too intense for your sensitive clit."

I followed his directions and waited.

"Now touch yourself."

My face flushed as I tentatively slid the vibrating object between my legs.

I gasped the second the vibrator came in contact with my sex. Arousal and need pulsed to life, soaking my pussy. I threw my head back, squeezing my eyes and legs closed.

"Spread those thighs. You don't get to hide anything from me."

There was an edge to his order that had me obeying.

"Circle the tip up and down your cunt. Keep doing it until I tell you otherwise."

"Hagen," I moaned.

A tingle shot up the base of my spine and everything inside me clenched. I bit my lips as my eyes closed tight.

I was almost there.

"Stop."

"What?" I gasped, holding the Lily against my clit.

He couldn't be serious.

"Starlight. I said stop."

A whimper escaped my mouth. "I need to come."

"Oh baby, you don't get to come for a little while yet. This is only the beginning."

"I don't understand."

"You wanted me, the dark and dirty. You're going to get it."

He walked over to me, his hard, thick cock building in his pants.

Crouching down, he set his hand over mine and moved the vibrator, positioning it on my thigh. The device pulsed against my skin but did nothing to elevate the desire to come.

With his other hand, he tugged the cups of my bra down and exposed my aching breasts to the cooling night air. He leaned forward, blew against one distended tip a second before he bit down.

"Ahh," I cried out, grabbing Hagen's shoulder and arching into the exquisite torture.

The pain was incredible and overwhelming and almost

too much. My pussy dripped from the pleasure-pain, and just as the delicious sting became bearable, he pulled away and moved to the other breast.

Fuck. Why did I like this so much?

My mind clouded with the need to run away and to tug him closer.

My juices soaked my thighs, and my pussy began to quicken. My back bowed up, letting the need for release merge with the agony of his bite. I was so turned on that I thought I'd shatter into a million pieces.

He freed my nipple and gave me a wicked grin.

"I thought," I said through pants, "you weren't into kink."

"No, I said I wasn't into the kink Pierce preferred. I don't need the extras. As you see, my mouth can garner the same reaction a pair of clamps can achieve."

I had no response to his statement. Up until now, he'd been dominant in bed but never anything like this. There was an edge to him that had me craving more.

His gaze slid between my legs and to the arousal soaking my cleft.

"Perfect."

He took my hand that held the vibrator and pressed it against my labia. The sensation was too much—I bucked and tried to move away. The orgasm came up on me so fast. My mind and body were screaming for release.

"Oh God. Oh God. Haaa...gen."

All of a sudden, he pulled the vibrator from my fingers and set it on the spa ledge.

Not again.

"No. Please," I begged.

"Do you want to come, baby?"

"Y...yes." My breath was coming in pants, and my fingers dug into the surround of the spa.

"Then you should have listened when I told you to stay quiet. Now you aren't allowed to come until I give you permission."

"I have no control over it."

"Yes, you do, baby. Plus, if you come there will be consequences."

Before I could wrap my mind around his words, his mouth descended and latched onto my swollen clit.

"Oh fuck, Hagen," I screamed.

He circled and laved my sensitive bud. He feasted on me, bringing me to the cusp over and over.

The last almost-orgasm had tears of frustration and need sliding down my cheeks. I was feverish, damp with sweat, and desperate for a release I knew he wouldn't give me.

"I hate you."

"No, you don't. You're just frustrated." He stared into

my eyes. "What you feel for me is more than a man like me should wish for or deserve."

He kissed the top of my head and the irritation with his refusal to let me come disappeared.

I was in love with this man. This flawed man with a tainted past.

I cupped his cheek and lifted my lips to his. Our kiss started soft and gentle, growing to all-consuming and desperate. I couldn't get enough of him.

My fingers slid between us to the opening of his shirt. I needed to feel him skin to skin. I had barely worked the first button undone when Hagen stayed my hands.

He reached to the side, picking up the Lily. "I want you to finish while I watch. I want to see your eyes glaze over as you come. Then I want to fill you until you come again."

My mouth grew parched at the raw desire in his gaze.

He placed the vibrator in my palm and then rose, returning to his seat.

This time there was no apprehension as I brought the device to my slick cleft. I began by gliding it up and down my sex and then pressed down against the tight bundle of nerves at the apex of my pussy.

I imagined it was Hagen's hands stroking me, bringing me pleasure, owning my body's response.

I cupped my breasts as the desire grew stronger and I felt the first tremors erupt in my core.

I rolled the vibrator around my clit while pinching my nipples. My pussy wept from the pleasure as sweat slid down my neck.

"Hagen," I screamed. "May I come?"

I wasn't sure why I asked for permission, but I knew it was the right thing to do.

There was a tug of satisfaction on the corners of his lips. "Yes, baby. Let go. Come for me."

Immediately my release washed over me. "Oh God, Hagen."

I bucked and arched against my own hand. My swollen tissue contracted over and over as I squeezed my eyes tight.

"That was fucking beautiful."

Panting to catch my breath, I opened my clamped eyes and looked at Hagen. His face was a play of lust, need, and something I wasn't sure I was reading correctly.

Before I pondered too long, I slid down from the hot tub surround and crawled to where Hagen sat.

I lifted onto my knees, pushing him back in his chair. Next, I glided my palms up his thighs, slowly molding my hand over the hard, straining cock under the fabric of his pants.

"I want him in my mouth."

"Then take him out." His raspy voice went straight to my aching pussy, igniting the desire that had barely been quenched by my orgasm from seconds earlier.

I licked my lips and followed his directive, undoing his belt and opening his button before sliding the zipper down. Immediately, his beautiful, thick length popped out from the opening in his boxers and slapped against his stomach.

He gripped the base, pumping up and down. "Hands behind your back."

I threaded my fingers along the base of my spine and waited. My mouth watered to taste him. A bead of precum glistened on the tip.

"Take me all the way back, as I taught you."

He held his ridged length for me, and I lowered, engulfing him deeply, until he hit the back of my throat. I swallowed, contracting the back of my throat so as not to choke.

As I lifted my head, I licked the thick vein under his erection.

"That's it, Starlight. Suck my cock."

I began a slow, steady rhythm, bobbing up and down.

After a few strokes, a low, guttural sound escaped Hagen's lips. Peeking up, I saw his head thrown back and his eyes clenched tight.

I continued my slow ministrations on his beautiful, thick cock, enjoying his deep groans and moans. His breath grew ragged and his fingers threaded into my hair. I felt the familiar swelling of his cock. I prepared myself for his release. I loved the taste of him and the raw way he'd come.

"Stop," he said, almost sounding as if he was in excruciating pain. "I don't want to come unless I'm buried deep in your pussy."

I ignored him, engulfing him deep and then contracting the back of my throat.

A sharp sting fired across my ass, making me gasp, and my pussy flood with arousal.

"I said stop." He tugged my head back and lifted me onto his lap.

He spread my legs apart, positioning the angry bulbous head of his erection at my weeping opening.

"Ride me."

I slid down his length and rose and lowered, letting him control the pace. With each glide down, he'd thrust upward.

We kissed and lost ourselves in each other.

It was raw, nothing like any time before.

As our orgasms rose, our movement grew unsteady, and his thrusts became harder.

I stared into his eyes, and without thinking, I said, "I love you."

He cupped the back of my head and ran a thumb over my lip and then down my throat. "I know. I've always known."

"I'm glad one of us was aware of it."

He smiled and pulled me against him as he pumped into my quivering pussy.

"Hagen, I'm close."

"I know. But before you go over, I have to make something clear."

"This isn't the time for a discussion. It's the time for fucking." I bore down on his cock as he drove up.

He lifted me, so I no longer had leverage.

"What are you doing?"

He ignored me and pushed his girth deep.

"You will never put yourself between me and someone who threatens your safety."

Thrust.

"You will protect what's mine."

Thrust.

"If anything happens to you, I will not hesitate to become the devil people believe me to be."

Thrust.

"You are mine."

Thrust, thrust.

"Do I make myself clear?"

Thrust.

My mind whirled with the depth of emotion in his words.

He stopped moving, making me cry out.

"I didn't hear your answer."

I clutched his shoulders. "Hagen, please. I'm almost there."

"No. Not until you answer me."

"Yes, I hear you. I'm yours. I'm yours. I've always been yours."

With the next thrust, we both erupted.

CHAPTER SEVENTEEN

Hagen

AROUND TWO IN THE MORNING, I gave up on trying to sleep. Starlight slept peacefully against my chest, and for the first time in my life, it felt like there was a person out there who was mine.

Hearing her tell me she loved me was indescribable. It also scared the shit out of me. For years, I'd known she had feelings for me. Just as I'd known I had to stay away from her.

She was all that was good and decent. And I was soiled by a hard life that had me involved in more than one situation that, if found out, could land me in jail for the rest of my life, or worse, dead.

I'd gotten out of that life, but it had this way of following me. Dealing with Kapok was only one of a long line of incidences where I'd had to rely on my old skills to handle things.

It had taken every fucking microscopic speck of my strength not to kill Kapok when he called Starlight a whore. The fucker wouldn't be messing with Starlight again.

Instead of shooting him and dumping his body as my instincts had screamed to do, I'd had a long chat with Kapok's boss, Josef Petrov. Petrov was the Russian version of Draco. They were friends inasmuch as two monsters could be friends. There was a mutual respect of each other and their territories—Vegas being Draco's.

Petrov knew my ties to Draco were as solid as ever, and an insult to me was one to Draco. The fact Kapok had insulted Starlight made it very clear that an unforgettable slight had occurred, especially since Starlight was favored by Draco. Petrov assured me that he'd take care of Kapok, which meant Kapok was being shipped, either to Siberia or to the afterlife.

I should've felt some remorse for essentially orchestrating Kapok's death sentence. But the bastard had gone out of his way to hurt Starlight.

And no one fucking hurt Starlight.

Next on the list was Dara, but my plan required Adrian's cooperation.

I glanced at Starlight's limp, satiated body draped over mine and felt my cock go from death to full salute.

This woman was mine.

Shit.

When had I started believing she could truly be mine? She had this way about her that kept me on my toes. She was nothing like I'd pegged her to be. She was far bolder and more daring than I could ever imagine. She was everything I could want in a woman.

I knew I'd said she was the only one who could break us up, but that hadn't meant I wouldn't kidnap her to convince her otherwise.

She owned a piece of my soul, she always had. I'd wanted her before she truly understood what a man like me craved.

She made me wish I was a better man, someone deserving of her, and for some reason she didn't see my faults.

Starlight shifted, and I held in a groan as her naked thigh grazed my straining dick. All I'd have to do was shift her and bury myself deep inside her delicious cunt.

No. I'd taken her hard. She needed the rest.

I gently moved her to the pillow next to me and rolled

out of bed. After draping the covers over her beautiful body, I walked into the living room.

Picking up my phone, I began to skim the messages that had come through over the past few hours. Most were updates from the various clubs, but then my gaze landed on one that had me pausing.

Collin Lykaios.

What the hell did the man want?

I hadn't spoken to him in years, and now he was contacting me?

I tapped his name and couldn't believe what I was reading.

Collin: Son, we need to talk. There are things we need to discuss. There are too many mistakes I've made for you to forgive me. I only hope you will hear me out and let me do something to protect the one person you care about most.

Starlight.

I dialed Collin's number, not caring it was two in the morning.

Collin answered on the first ring. "Son."

I clenched my teeth. He'd never called me that—*idiot, disappointment,* and *a waste of space* were his usual M.O.

"What do you need to say?"

There was a sigh. "Dara contacted me as a buyer for Kipos."

"That's not news. She contacted us too."

"Don't buy it, no matter what. And for God's sake, don't let Persephone sign anything to sell it."

"Why not?" I ran a frustrated hand over my face and stared into the night.

"Dara is under investigation for using the company as a means to transport illegal plant products into Europe and the United States, meaning drugs."

"Fuck. She's trying to set Starlight up to take the fall for the company. That's why she fired her."

"Yes. You were only an excuse."

"How do you know all this?"

"I can't reveal my sources."

"Of course, you can't."

His voice grew solemn. "Son. I—"

"Stop calling me that," I snapped. "I haven't been that for fifteen years. Now cut to the chase and tell me why you feel the need to protect me and what's mine."

"I made mistakes with all three of you, but most of all you. My only excuse was that I let circumstances in my life rule how I reacted with you boys. I'm ashamed of how I handled things with you."

"Yeah, throwing a rebellious seventeen-year-old out onto the streets was a great reaction to drinking with his friends underaged."

"I looked for you every day for months, but you

disappeared. No matter who I contacted, they couldn't help me. I nearly went out of my mind with worry. I swear to you that I regretted what happened immediately."

"Bullshit. I lived in shelters for three months before Draco found me."

"Draco hid you until he had you desperate enough to go work for him. When I found out, I did everything in my power to get you back. But by then you were in his world and he viewed you as the payment for the debt I owed him. I let you go because I had no choice. It was the only way to protect you and your brothers."

"Let me repeat. That's bullshit. Draco was more of a father to me than you ever were."

"Ask him." The sound of ice clinking in a glass echoed over the line. "Draco will admit what he did."

"If that's true, then what did he have on you that he'd retaliate by taking me?"

"It's no longer important. I'll let you go. Just know that old age has taught me family is the most important thing in a man's life."

Collin hung up.

What the fuck just happened?

I had to get to the bottom of this.

Hagen

A COUPLE OF HOURS LATER, I entered one of Draco's private clubs and headed directly to where he held court tonight. A group of men were in the middle of an animated discussion as scantily clad women sat on their laps.

Draco saw me approach.

"Hagen, this is a surprise."

"*Oyabun*, we need to talk."

He lifted a brow at the edge in my voice, but instead of saying anything, he nodded and rose without a word to the group around him.

After we entered the private office, he turned to study me.

"Tell me it isn't true."

"First you need to tell me what we are discussing."

"Did Collin try to find me? Did you make it impossible for him? Did you plan to take me the second you heard about my fight with Collin? Did you force his hand in how he handled my brothers?"

Draco moved to a long sofa against the dark mahogany walls.

"Yes. You were payment for a debt your father refused to pay me."

"And my brothers? Did you make Collin destroy Pierce and Zack's childhoods too?"

"I wouldn't say destroy, but it was more that I influenced him to sever ties with his precious sons to protect his eldest and clear the debt he owed me."

It took all my strength not to sway at the slap of the answer.

"What was the debt?"

"One of his partners, Victor Anthony, swindled me out of nearly fifty million. I required payment for the debt, and your father stood in the way."

I had a feeling I knew what he was about to tell me.

"You were going to take Anthony's daughters as payment. For prostitution?"

The thought of what would have happened to Henna and Anaya made my stomach turn. He would have destroyed the beautiful, intelligent women they were by exposing them to the world of prostitution.

I'd never liked focusing on the darker side of Draco's business, prostitution being a big part of it. I'd worked for him for years and had gotten so much shit for avoiding that aspect of Draco's business. Now I was thankful for my choice.

"No, I only required one. And again no, the girl would have been a companion to my granddaughter. She was lonely as the only girl among so many boys. Eventually,

Anthony's daughter would have married one of my grandsons, and the debt would be complete. The girl wouldn't have had a hard life. Besides, I wasn't the only one after Anthony's family as payment for his betrayal. If others had gotten their hands on either of the girls, more than likely they'd have been dead. I was the better option all around."

"I still don't understand. How did Collin stand in the way?"

"He hid the girls and their mother. They'd disappeared until a few years ago. Do you realize how different your life would have been if only Collin had chosen between the older girl and the one who belonged to your mother?"

The confusion must have shown on my face because he continued. "Don't tell me you had no idea that your mother had a long-running affair with Anthony? Zacharias is not Rhea's youngest child. Anaya Anthony is."

Hagen

I WALKED through the next few days in a daze. I avoided all contact with Starlight or my brothers. Instead, I immersed myself in the last-minute logistics of Ida's grand opening.

It helped that Starlight's team had arrived and kept her company for the most part. The reports I had gotten said she had each of the women roped into moonlighting as lab assistants.

The only time I had any contact with Starlight was when I buried my cock deep inside her when I'd finish for the night with the clubs. She'd be in bed sleeping, always naked, always ready for me.

Avoiding Zack and Pierce was another story. We ran multiple businesses together. Therefore, I'd resorted to emails, text messages, and having my managers go to meetings.

I knew I was a pussy, but how does one tell his brothers that the mother we'd idolized had had a long-running affair with our father's best friend and then given birth to our sister during the time she'd left us with *Yia Yia* for five months to travel the world with her friends?

I had no doubt in my mind Draco had told me the truth. He had no need to lie. He always said the reality is more lethal than fabrications.

Draco's admission had damaged something between us. Collin hadn't abandoned me as I'd believed. I'd been a pawn to Draco. It was just the luck of the draw that Draco grew attached to me and decided to raise me as he did his children and grandchildren.

Then, if my fucked-up family life wasn't enough shit on my shoulders, I had to tell Penny she couldn't sell Kipos, no matter what.

God, I hoped Adrian had his plans in order. He needed to know what was happening under his mother's watch. The crazy part was he hadn't seemed fazed when I'd relayed what Collin had discovered. It was more like he was annoyed.

"Here's another, Mr. Lykaios." The bartender pushed a tumbler in my direction as I sat at a hidden bar in the Nyx nightclub.

I sipped my drink and watched the club dancers get into position for the guest DJ who'd host tonight's events at the club. The place was packed from celebrities to high rollers.

A text came through on my phone.

Starlight: If you don't come up here and tell me what the fuck is going on with you, I swear I will leave. It takes two people for a relationship, and from where I see it, you don't want to be in one.

Immediately another came in.

Starlight: I get that you're freaked out that I said I loved you but avoiding me for five fucking days is not the way to handle it. You either come up here this minute, or

I'm packing my bags and heading to Henna's. She moved into her new condo, and she has plenty of room for me.

I cringed. I was in for it.

Wait a second, did she say she was leaving me?

The hell she was.

She was the one woman who challenged me, surprised me, and made me feel more than I ever knew I could.

I pushed back from the bar and tried to maneuver around a few enthusiastic patrons.

One smiled in my direction while her friends ordered the signature cocktail for the evening, the Fiery Night.

"Hey, aren't you Hagen Lykaios?"

I didn't confirm but said, "Have a good night, ladies."

Another women blocked my way, setting a hand on my chest. "Remember me, stranger? It's been a long time."

I groaned inside. I'd dated, no, fucked, Pamala Green about five years ago. She was a well-known fashion model who'd made headlines for all her high-profile relationships with wealthy men. Me being one of them.

She was one of the few exes I avoided at all costs. She was clingy and an all-around headache. Outside of the fact she was pretty to look at, she was a complete bitch.

The last thing I needed was for Starlight to see Pamala hanging onto me. It would make the shithole I was swimming in ten times worse.

"Come on, sexy. You remember we were good together. I can show you a really good time."

Typically I'd have been a bit gentler, but I had priorities and she wasn't one of them.

I jerked Pamala's hand from my body. "Thank you for the offer, but I have a girlfriend."

"I saw your pictures in the newspaper. She's pretty but not your usual type. More on the homely side, not the type of outgoing woman you need."

I glared at her, not wanting to act on the urge to throw her out of my club. "Good night, Pamala. I'm sure you can find someone else to keep you company."

"She doesn't have to know." Pamala batted her eyelashes, stepping in my path.

What the fuck had I seen in this woman?

"I'd know." My voice grew cold. "And I don't cheat. Now I suggest you enjoy the club with your friends while I take care of other matters."

I walked around Pamala and her friends but came to an abrupt halt.

Starlight stood a few feet from me. She wasn't looking at me but shooting daggers at Pamala behind me.

"Starlight." I moved into her line of sight, slid one hand around her waist, and kissed her forehead. "I was just coming up."

"I can see that."

I picked up her clenched fist and kissed her knuckles. "Let's go home, baby."

She stayed quiet as we left the club and the whole way back to our home.

As we entered the penthouse, I knew without a doubt the incident at the club hadn't helped her anger.

I moved to the bar, poured two fingers of Firewater Reserve and shot it back, letting the smooth liquid warm my body.

Setting the glass down, I turned. "Starlight. I fucked up again."

She stared at me and without a word came toward me, pushing me back against the wall with a palm to my throat, and covered my mouth with hers.

I reacted without thinking and met her demands with my own. I pushed my tongue past her lips, drowning in her sweet taste.

"You're mine. Do I make myself clear? I do not share," she gritted out and trailed her cheek along my stubble-covered jaw like a cat leaving her scent.

"Is that so?"

She pulled back, eyes blazing a piercing green that almost looked black.

"Did I stutter?"

If that's how she wanted to play, then we'd play. Before she could move, I reversed our positions and had her pinned to the glass wall with the Vegas sky behind us.

Surprise crossed her face, as did unbridled lust.

"Let me make something clear to you. No one touches you either. I own you."

Temper flared in her gaze, and she responded by biting my lower lip and drawing blood. "Then that better mean I'm the only one who fucks you or gets to take you home for a good time."

"Is that an ultimatum?"

My girl was jealous. If she only knew the only woman I saw was her.

"Yes," she bit out. "You're not the only one who's possessive."

I couldn't help but smile.

How had the situation gone from me preparing to grovel to this? I knew better than to question luck when it appeared.

"Don't laugh at me. I'm serious," she growled and tried to bite my lip again.

I was too quick for her and had her hair in an unyielding hold.

I jerked her head back. "You want to play rough, Starlight. We can play rough."

"Give it your best shot," she bit out as desire flushed her golden skin.

"With pleasure." I lifted her against my body, not loosening my grip on her hair.

We kissed like people starved for each other.

Fuck, this woman was everything I could ever want.

I carried her to our bedroom, letting her slide down when we neared the bed.

She pushed at my shirt, pulling it over my head. I had to get my hands on her. So instead of waiting to touch her skin, I tore her dress down the center. The pieces of scrap fell to the floor, revealing a curvy body I couldn't get enough of.

I walked forward, making her retreat, and just as the backs of her knees were about to hit the bed, I turned her, tumbling her onto her front.

I pulled her hips up and back until she was on all fours.

God, that ass. My cock would take her there soon.

Ripping her thong, I climbed onto the bed behind her as I shoved my pants to my knees.

Immediately, I slid my cock between the velvety heat of her soaked pussy lips.

A low, guttural moan escaped my lips, and it was killing me not to sink balls-deep.

"Starlight. This is sweet heaven."

I rubbed the angry head of my cock from the entrance

of her juicy cunt to her sensitive swollen clitoral nub and then back again.

"Hagen, please. Fuck me already. I want it hard. I want to feel you with every step tomorrow."

Her words ignited a feral need I couldn't control.

I reached over to the bedside table and grabbed the tie I'd left there last night.

"You want it rough?" I pulled her hands behind her back and tied them together with the silk. "You want it hard?" I grabbed her hair, tugging her head back while positioning my cock at her cunt. "You want to feel me with every step you take?"

"Yes. Dammit. Yes. I want it all. Don't hold back. I won't break."

I gripped her hip and slammed into her, forcing both of us forward.

"Haagggen," she moaned as I set an unrelenting pace.

I fucked her harder than I'd fucked anyone in my life.

I knew my hold on her was painful, but she seemed to love it, and it pushed me to keep up the hard, demanding thrusts.

Her pussy wept and began to quiver around my cock.

I pulled her up and against my front while continuing to pummel her cunt. Her arms were trapped between our bodies. Having her helpless and entirely under my control was a heady feeling, and the fact she had complete trust in me spurred my desire for her.

"Who do you belong to, Starlight?"

"You. Only you," she answered without hesitation, and I knew I'd just sealed my fate with this woman.

"Now make me come," she ordered.

I couldn't help but laugh and give her what she wanted.

CHAPTER EIGHTEEN

Penny

"I THINK YOU KILLED ME," Hagen said into my hair.

His body weight pushed me into the mattress, and his hand still gripped my hair.

I loved the feel of him on me, but my bound arms were beginning to go numb.

"You're not the one with a hundred-and-ninety-pound man on top of you."

He shifted, his cock slipping from my body. Almost immediately a stream of hot semen coated my thighs. Hagen reached to the bedside table, grabbed a facial tissue, and wiped me. Once I was clean, he untied my arms and rubbed the feeling back into them before pulling me back onto his hard chest.

Now that I'd gotten my jealousy out of my system, it was time to get to the bottom of his mood over the past few days.

"Want to tell me what happened?"

He sighed and threw a hand over his head. "I learned some news that will affect all of us. Let's say I didn't handle it well."

I rolled to my side and leaned over him. "That's an understatement. You froze all of us out. And don't say fucking me senseless when you got in bed counts as keeping things hot."

"I'm sorry." He paused. "The news is pretty shocking."

"As long as we're not related, I think we're good."

The thought of that made me shudder. Yes, I was half Greek, but no one wants to be part of any Greek tragedy.

"You have no idea how close your statement is."

"What? I think you need to start at the beginning."

"Then that would start with the text from Collin the night Kapok decided to cause havoc."

Hagen relayed his conversation with Collin, and I couldn't let the anger of the situation get to me.

"She was setting me up to take the fall while she disappeared with Papa's money? I hate her for so many things, but this takes the cake.

"Dammit, I'd resigned myself to selling and even giving Dara her share would be fine, but this. I'm damned if I do and damned if I don't."

Hagen rubbed my bare back. "It'll work out."

"I have to tell Adrian." I glanced at the bedside table. "Shit, my phone's in the living room."

I moved to slide from the bed, but Hagen caught me around the waist, hurling me back to him.

"He already knows."

I folded my arms across my chest. "Of course, he does. You talk to him but not me or your brothers."

"Adrian is going to come to see you later to explain. Listen to him."

"The timing is interesting."

"Meaning?"

"Dara's attorney sent a packet for me to review. She has a buyer for Kipos. They want me to go in on Monday to sign the papers."

"She's desperate since Adrian's birthday is at the end of next week and he gains control of his portion of the company."

"My gut was telling me not to sign even if it was for the good of the company anyway, but now after what you told me, I'm determined to avoid the meeting altogether."

"I think you should go." Hagen glided his hand up and down my back.

I glared. "Why?"

"Adrian will explain everything."

I hated waiting. Dammit. I hated not having control.

Taking a deep breath, I said, "I swear one day I am going to kick both your and Adrian's asses for keeping secrets from me."

He lifted a brow. "Woman, you have more secrets than nearly anyone I know."

"Whatever, just keep me in the loop from now on," I muttered. "Now want to tell me the real reason you ghosted me this week."

"I wasn't ghosting you. If I were ghosting you, I wouldn't have come home to our bed every night. I'd have stayed in the apartment above the club."

"Then what is it?"

"I have a sister." His voice grew grim, and sadness entered his eyes.

"A what?" I sat up. "Okay, I think we need to start from the beginning."

"There was something else that Collin said that had me questioning the past."

I kept quiet, letting him process his thoughts.

"Collin said he looked for me for months. He said Draco hid me as a way to get back at him. And he told me to get the truth from Draco."

"Where does the sister come in?"

"I confronted Draco, and he admitted that he kept me from my family. He hid me because Collin hid Henna and Anaya. Victor Anthony had swindled Draco out of millions, and one of the girls was going to be payment for what your uncle did."

Bile rose in my throat.

"Collin saved their lives by giving them new identities and moving them to Colorado. Collin refused to pick between his goddaughter and his wife's daughter."

It took me a second to understand what he'd said. Anaya was Rhea's daughter. Meaning Uncle Victor had had an affair with her twenty years ago.

When I looked into Hagen's eyes, I knew I'd drawn the correct conclusion.

"How long did the affair last?"

"Not sure, but from what Draco said, it was ongoing for years."

There was distaste in his voice as he used Draco's name. I could only imagine how he felt—the man he viewed as the enemy his whole life had made mistakes with him but hadn't betrayed him as he believed. And the man he'd loved as his surrogate father was the enemy, or close to it.

"Draco orchestrated everything I went through on the streets to make me desperate enough to beg for any bone he threw at me. I can't describe the shit that happened to me." He squeezed his eyes tight and gripped his hair, releasing a pained breath.

I cupped his face in my hands. "You don't have to talk about it. I get it."

"Do you think Henna or Anaya know?"

I shook my head. "They would have told me. We've never kept anything from each other. They both carry the shame of what Uncle Victor did like a heavy chain around their neck. If it hadn't been for my aunt, they would have kept their assumed names instead of using their real ones when they came back to Nevada."

"Makes sense."

A thought crossed my mind as I studied Hagen's face and remembered Anaya's.

"Why are you looking at me like that?"

I traced my thumb down the bridge of his nose and then over his lips. "I just realized how much you and Ana resemble each other. I always thought her super-fair skin came from the northern Indian side of Uncle Victor's family, but now it makes sense."

"Starlight, you can't tell anyone. Henna and Anaya have built a life for themselves and don't need the scandal. And my brothers." Hagen sighed. "Pierce will take it and move forward, but Zack. I'm not sure how he'll handle it. It would kill him to know Mama wasn't the angel he believed her to be."

I dropped my head to his chest. "What are we going to do?"

"We?"

"Yes, we."

He released a deep sigh, and for the first time since we started talking, the stress eased. "I like the sound of that."

"Now answer the question."

"First, we need to handle the situation with Dara. Then we'll tackle the other issue."

"And how do we handle the Dara situation without making it so I don't go to jail?" I asked, as I peered up at him.

"That's where your brother comes in. He's working at the Aegis until midnight, so he'll be over after his shift."

I glanced at the clock. "That's two hours from now. I'm not sure I can wait that long to hear your plan."

"Did you ever hear the phrase 'patience is a virtue'?"

"Isn't it obvious? I don't have any. What am I going to do for the next two hours? I don't like watching TV, and I left my eReader in the lab."

He pushed me onto my back and pulled my legs around his waist. "I'm sure I can think of a few things to occupy your time. I have a bit more making up to do."

Penny

"THE WALLFLOWER IS GONE, Persephone. You are not going to let her push you around anymore," I said to myself as I stared at my reflection in the hallway mirror of Hagen's condo...umm...*my* condo.

I couldn't believe how much had changed in a matter of weeks. I was no longer the Kipos heiress but the Firewater mogul. Tonight, the world would learn I was the creator of the coveted whiskey.

It was all part of Adrian's plan.

After Adrian had come to the penthouse a few days earlier, we'd agreed that it was time for me to come out as the owner of PSK Distilleries. Dara was using a potential contract with PSK as a selling feature for Kipos. She needed to see that unless she played nice with me, there would be no selling Kipos International to anyone.

For now, I'd let her believe she had the upper hand. Adrian and I both knew her pride and ego went hand in hand, and she viewed framing me for her illegal activities as a boon to her agenda.

On Monday, I'd play my ace and see her world crumble around her.

My heart still ached, knowing I probably would never get to the truth behind Papa's death. Hagen said none of the investigators had any leads, and his relationship with Draco had cooled, making me hesitant to ask Hagen to contact him.

Maybe it was better not to know. It wouldn't bring Papa back, and both Adrian and I had lives away from Kipos.

Adrian had agreed to sell the company as soon as we cleaned up the mess Dara had created, but it required Adrian to turn twenty-one, and that wasn't for a few more days.

"Are you still brooding?" Adrian asked as he walked in.

He wore a custom-tailored tuxedo, and he'd tamed his normally shaggy hair, making him look like he just walked off the pages of a fashion magazine.

"You clean up nicely, baby bro."

"Thank you. You look beautiful yourself. Though I'm not sure if that is supposed to be a dress or a swimsuit with a sheer skirt."

"Ha-ha. You think you're funny. Henna had it made for me when she was in Italy. It's haute couture."

The second Henna had brought it over last night I knew the men in my life would have a multitude of objections to the ensemble. The body of the dress was the reddish brown of Firewater, and the transparent fabric that made up the skirt had pale hues of silver and rose gold. It was nothing like the sensible Persephone Kipos would have worn in the past, but this dress fit my style better than any other gown I'd worn in public before.

"It wouldn't matter if it was vintage and worth a hundred grand. The second Hagen sees it, he's going to lose his shit."

"He isn't going to be here tonight, so we have nothing to worry about."

About two hours ago, Hagen had called saying he was delayed with a major build-out error at a new club and that it would be virtually impossible for him to get back in time for my introduction and the announcement of the deal I'd negotiated with Zack for the exclusive distribution of Firewater Incognito to the Lykaios brothers.

When Adrian had proposed the possibility, I'd balked. But then after I thought about it, I knew he was right. Having Zack handle the marketing and distribution of the new whiskey would take some of the tasks I hated off my shoulders.

"I wouldn't count on that. Hagen will be here sooner or later. And there are bound to be pictures in the entertainment news channels. This place is packed with celebrities."

I glared at Adrian through the mirror. "Hagen has no say in what I wear. Plus, I think I look hot."

"No comment on that statement. We're Greek and all, but that's not something I like to consider my sister as."

Adrian picked up a shot of Firewater and downed it. He closed his eyes, enjoying the burn of the liquor.

I turned. "Excuse me, but you haven't turned twenty-one yet. Don't get caught drinking in public. There will be cameras everywhere, and we don't need Dara causing you any grief."

"Speaking of Mommy Dearest. Are you okay with the plan?"

"I'm not going to lie. After all we did to keep Papa's legacy, it feels like Dara won. We still don't have a clear picture of how she was involved in Papa's death."

"Think about it this way: we will get her one way or the other. Focus on the fact that she will be out of your life for good by the end of the day on Monday."

I sighed and said, "I am, but in the end, she'll always be your mother."

Adrian shook his head. "Dara Kipos may have given birth to me, but she isn't my mother. My mother is the woman I'm looking at right now."

My lips trembled, and tears burned the backs of my eyes.

"You were a kid yourself, but you put your dreams aside to raise me. I know the truth even if no one else does." Adrian pulled me into his arms and squeezed me close.

I held on to him and soaked in his warmth. Adrian was what had kept me going all these years. If it hadn't been for how much he needed me, I'd have probably given up. He had done for me as much as I'd done for him.

Reaching into his back pocket, Adrian pulled out a handkerchief and dabbed at my face.

"No more tears or thinking about the past. It's time to focus on you and the future you are creating. Plus, you'll ruin your makeup, and you know how Camellia gets when anyone messes up her creations."

I sniffed. "I love you, sweet boy."

"Boy?" He pulled back with a fake frown. "I'm no boy. I'm a man."

Laughing, I gave him one last squeeze before I returned to the mirror to make sure my eye makeup wasn't smudged.

"Oh, by the way, I have a present for you from a man who hoped to give it to you himself."

My heart skipped a beat.

Adrian reached into the inside pocket of his tuxedo jacket and pulled out a long rectangular box. He opened it and revealed a thin white diamond necklace with a pink diamond pendant in the shape of an elderflower.

"Oh my." I gingerly touched the gems.

"I'm happy you finally found a man as in love with you as you are with him."

"He's not in love with me. He wants me and cares for me, but it's not love."

I wanted to believe Hagen loved me but I was too afraid to hope. The statements of me keeping him and saying only I could end us made me think he might love me. But I needed to hear the words no one had given me before.

Adrian opened the clasp and set the necklace against my collarbone before fastening it.

"You may not see it, but I do. He's in love with you. He's not the type of man to declare it with words, but he does love you."

"I suppose." The weight of the necklace was significantly heavier than I expected.

There was a note in the box.

Starlight,

I had this made for you. It is rare and unique like you.

No more hiding in the shadows.

Hagen

"As I said, the man is a goner over you."

At that moment the elevator doors opened, and Zack stepped out with Pierce right behind him.

"Let's go, beautiful." Zack nodded to Adrian and tucked my arm into the crook of his elbow. "Time to get everyone drunk on your thousand-dollar-an-ounce lab experiment."

"Ha-ha, you should consider becoming a comedian if this real-estate thing doesn't work out."

Penny

I WALKED onto Hagen's private balcony overlooking Ida's opulent ballroom about two hours after the official opening of the hotel and presenting myself as the reclusive owner of Firewater. I found a spot in the shadows, away from the light of the hotel and took a calming breath.

I was feeling a bit overwhelmed and hoped to get a few moments without anyone fawning over Firewater or giving me advice on my business. I knew everyone meant well, but no matter what they believed, I wasn't the naive girl they knew.

The reaction of the party attendees and media was a mix of curiosity and speculation. From the little bits I kept hearing all night, most of the public believed I was ousted from Kipos due to a conflict of interest. However, others made not-so-subtle comments about Dara's jealousy of me and the need to get me away from her son's inheritance. It surprised me how many people didn't like Dara, even though she "lunched" with many of them.

Overall, the night had gone better than I expected— well, outside of one irritation.

Dara.

In spite of Adrian saying we needed her to come to the opening, in the back of my mind, I'd hoped she'd decline. Dara had a hard-and-fast rule never to attend any event hosted by the Lykaios brothers. But of course, she decided today was the day to show up. And I knew it was because of me.

Earlier in the day, a gossip magazine published pictures of Hagen and me from the night of the poker game and Kapok's rude appearance. The images were of Hagen holding me close against him in the casino, and then others of us eating pastries at the hotel's patisserie.

The headline of the article said: "The Master of Sin and Indulgence Has Found His Angel."

I could only assume Dara wasn't happy with the attention my relationship with Hagen was getting.

It hadn't even taken ten minutes after entering the ballroom with Zack for Dara to approach us.

It was as if she was waiting until we arrived to make a beeline in our direction. I'd expected a confrontation but not before the announcement.

Her words had been full of venom when she'd spoken to me.

"I see how far you've fallen. Not only are you Hagen's whore, now you're with Zacharias. Your father would be ashamed of you. If you ruin the sale because of your antics, I'll make sure you regret it for the rest of your life."

Using Papa against me was the ultimate slap. This woman truly hated me. She would have never insulted me the way she had if Adrian was anywhere near. I'd had to dig my fingers into Zack's arm to keep him from responding. She'd wanted one of us to lash out and make a scene that the press could latch on to for the next morning's headlines. But instead I'd only lifted a brow and said, *"I suggest you don't make an enemy of me. Without my signature, you can't do anything with Kipos but run it into the ground."*

I'd walked away with my head held high. Then, when Zack had introduced me as the owner of PSK Distilleries and Firewater, I felt a surge of triumph when Dara's face grew deathly pale.

I set my champagne glass on the balcony ledge and closed my eyes as the breeze picked up, cooling my heated skin.

"I've never been so jealous of the wind before. I should be the only one allowed to put that look on your face."

CHAPTER NINETEEN

Hagen

STARLIGHT TURNED, and I nearly swallowed my tongue.

This woman was perfection incarnate. From the view I'd had of her from the back, she looked like a petite ballerina with her wispy dress and neatly styled bun. But from the front, she was a walking wet dream.

And what the hell was she wearing? It looked like an overly cleavage-baring leotard with a see-through skirt.

I was the only man allowed to see that body.

Heat flared in her eyes too as she took me in. My cock swelled, and I had visions of pinning her to the railing and fucking her senseless.

She gripped the railing behind her and leaned back. "The breeze is all I have. You've been a bit preoccupied the last two days. I had to get my kicks some way."

I lifted a brow as I walked toward her. "Is that right?"

The scent of light floral perfume mixed with her own unique essence reached my nose, making my need for her rise higher.

"I wasn't expecting you to be here until much later."

"You should know by now that nothing would keep me from you."

I could tell my words pleased her as a flush crept up her skin. "How was your trip? Did you resolve the crisis?"

"For the most part. I'm just happy my flight wasn't delayed leaving Arizona."

It was a near miss that I made it tonight. A storm had started rolling through the area around Tucson, and we'd barely made it through before the airport grounded all planes.

I wouldn't have even left Vegas if another of our construction managers hadn't quit. However, this time it wasn't because they were caught stealing. The manager's quick departure had to do with Draco getting involved. Draco wanted my attention, and shutting down a fifty-million-dollar project was his way of getting it.

I honestly wasn't sure I'd ever have been ready to talk to him if he hadn't forced me to meet with him. When it came to Draco, I'd always taken things head-on, but this time, the betrayal felt worse than what Collin had done to me and my brothers.

Draco had arrived at the construction site with five of his grandsons, all men I'd grown up with. And all men who knew what Draco had done while I was oblivious. He'd looked so fragile as he walked the property, making me realize that even though Draco looked younger than his seventy-five years, in fact, he was very old.

Meeting with him was better than dealing with more problems for HPZ. And I knew without a doubt, Draco would orchestrate the shutdown of every one of our projects to get his way. The conversation had been surprisingly easy, and in the end, I realized Draco had actually viewed me as another of his grandsons. He may not have had those expectations in the beginning, but I had the feeling that he regretted the past. Nothing could change what happened, but Draco agreed to give me full disclosure when it came to anything to do with my family or Starlight.

I wouldn't say all was forgiven, but we'd come to an understanding and could move on from there.

Now I had to take the step to talk to Collin. I owed him that much. Whatever his actions were toward his sons, he'd protected two innocent girls, one of them being the product of his wife's affair with his best friend.

But that was for another day and time.

Right now, my attention was on the nature goddess dressed in scraps of cloth disguised as a dress.

"Just for the record, I hate that dress. It shows off too much of what is mine." My hands went around her slim waist. "Remind me to tell Henna she isn't allowed to pick any more dresses for you."

"It's haute couture. I like it." She tried to give me a stern glare, but the breathiness of her voice gave away the arousal she felt with me near her.

"It's a barely there leotard with a completely see-through skirt."

"You know what else it is?"

My lips grazed her ear, eliciting an almost purr. "What?"

She shifted her face until our noses were almost touching. "Easy access."

My mouth quirked at the corners. "Anyone could come out here and find us."

"I've already been corrupted thoroughly. It would only add to the rumors that I was under the control of the Master of Sin."

"For the first time, I don't mind that stupid title."

I slowly lowered to my knees. "Hold on tight. I'm about to feast on your beautiful cunt and then once I'm done, we're going home so I can fuck you so hard my cock imprints itself in your pussy."

Her breath came out in shallow pants, and I could see her nipples pebble and strain through the thin silk of her gown.

My focus moved to the tiny swatch of fabric covering her crotch. Licking my lips, I slid my hand up the slit of skirt that ran from the bottom of one leg to the juncture of her bodysuit-covered pussy.

I pushed the sheer ivory fabric to the side.

"Now I see what you meant by easy access."

I snapped open the buttons holding the crotch closed, exposing her beautiful, glistening pussy. "God, you're so wet."

I slid my fingers through the slit of her soaked lower lips, spreading them until I exposed her swollen clitoral nub. I blew onto the sensitized flesh a second before my mouth descended, sucking the bundle of nerves into my mouth.

Fuck, I was in heaven. Nothing tasted as good as her arousal. It was like an addictive ambrosia.

Her body bowed as my tongue thrust deep into her soaked channel.

"Hagen," she moaned as her hands gripped the railing tighter. "Oh God, Hagen."

I needed to hear more of her pleasure. Grabbing the

backs of her thighs, I spread her legs wider and feasted on the delicious pussy. My tongue circled, licked, and flicked her dripping core.

"I love tasting you," I growled as I continued to devour her. "I will never stop craving you on my lips."

I pressed a finger into her slick heat, and her orgasm erupted.

"Oh, God. Yes." She moaned, biting her lip to keep from screaming her pleasure.

Her eyes squeezed tight, and she writhed under the pleasurable torture. Her swollen tissue spasmed and clamped down on my pistioning fingers, and her arousal flooded my mouth, making me want to prolong the ecstasy coursing through her. But I knew we had to stop.

Reluctantly I pulled from her body, licking my fingers and wiping my drenched mouth against her thigh, then refastened the snaps between her legs. Rising slowly to my feet, I pulled her against me.

Her head tumbled to my shoulder in satiated pleasure. "I can't believe we just did that."

" We're on a balcony the public can't access or see." I stared down at her dazed face. "We could have gone much further and no one would ever know."

God, she was beautiful.

"In that case." She gave me a wicked smile. "Let's do it again soon."

Penny

"JUST KEEP THINKING of your cunt wrapped around my cock," Hagen said with a smirk as I walked with him through the doors of Kipos International on Monday morning.

I elbowed him in the stomach. "You are so crude. Most women are offended by that word."

"Good thing you aren't one of them."

My cheeks heated. He was well aware that the dirtier he talked to me the more aroused I became.

"You're the one who wanted me to corrupt you." He ran a thumb across my lips, making a shiver run down my spine. "I plan to enjoy every moment we have together."

A look passed in his eyes that made my heart clench. It was as if he thought I was going to leave him.

"Hagen, is there something you're not telling me?"

"I..." He hesitated. "Forget it. We'll talk about it after the meeting."

Before I could argue, Jeffery, one of the longtime Kipos security leads, came toward us.

"Penny. It's good to see you." He kissed my cheek. "Are you really going to let her sell the company?"

I expected this question. I would sell the company today, just not to the bidder Dara had arranged.

"It's for the best," I said and then sighed as Papa's giant portrait came into view on one of the walls of the lobby.

I'm sorry Papa. But Kipos is your dream, not your children's. I hope you can understand.

"At least I can say I stayed with the company for its entire history." Jeffery gave me a melancholy smile and pushed the button to the elevator. "Head on up. They're in the large conference room."

The second the doors opened on the executive floor, Adrian appeared and began to speak. "When we go in, make sure you keep to script."

"Well, hello to you too," I said and moved past him. "I'm not an idiot."

"I didn't say you were." His defensive and defiant tone made me want to laugh.

No matter the fact he towered over me, he was still the baby brother rebelling against any criticism.

"Does she know Hagen's coming with me or is she expecting me alone?" I looked in Hagen's direction but asked Adrian the question.

"She knows one of the Lykaios brothers is always with you."

I'd said to Adrian it was better for Dara to continue the assumption that I was with all of the brothers. Going by the pissed-off glare Hagen was giving me now, he was still mad at me for the suggestion. But he knew it was necessary as part of the plan Adrian had concocted.

As we approached the glass-walled conference room, I noticed Dara with her attorney, Trey Ritchman, and the usual entourage of minions sitting on one side of the table. On the other end was Carter Jones, my attorney. He wasn't pleased I was selling but accepted my decision. As far as Carter knew, the newly discovered will would cement my and Adrian's claim to the company without the need for Dara. He'd gone as far as advising us to contact the board and oust Dara from her role as CEO.

What I couldn't tell him was that if we got rid of Dara, then I would be responsible for the mess Dara had made of the company.

Right before we entered the room, Hagen turned to me and said, "I'm here to support you, but this is your fight. Remember, no matter what Dara says, stay calm. Her goal is to hurt you. It's time you took the reins of your life, Starlight."

I nodded and held in the tears that burned the backs of my eyes. He truly accepted me. He knew this was something I had to handle.

Leaning up, I kissed his cheek. "I love you, Hagen Lykaios. Thanks for having my back."

"You're welcome." He gave me a shy smile.

He still hadn't told me he loved me, but I knew it was under there. For a man with a reputation as a cold-as-ice hardass, he rarely showed me that side of him. Outside of being a dominant lover, he was considerate, funny, and a romantic, even if he wouldn't admit it.

"Let's go, baby. Time to face the dragon." Hagen pushed the door open.

"She's finally here. Thought you were going to make us wait all morning. Take a seat and let's get to it." The sneer in Dara's voice almost made me flinch.

Almost.

"Sorry." I looked in Dara's direction and then at Hagen. "It was his fault."

Hagen smirked and lifted a brow as we moved to our seats.

"What is he doing here?"

Hagen answered, "I'm sure you've heard, I go where she goes."

"If you think to make her change her mind, I'd think twice. I won't let anyone mess with my son's future."

I nearly choked on her false sense of parental worry. Where was this concern when Adrian was a child?

"I'm only here as moral support. It's a shame to see what has become of Uncle Jacob's company. I guess the strip club industry doesn't teach one how to run a multinational organization." Hagen sat back in his seat.

When Hagen had told me all that he'd discovered about Dara's past, I nearly fell out of my chair. She'd been a topless dancer for years before she married her first husband, a car dealership owner who'd been one of her best customers. After that, she'd put on the persona of a super puritan and proper lady. That was probably what had lured Papa to her.

Surprise crossed Dara's face and then she glanced in my direction.

Yes, bitch. We know all your secrets.

"Let's begin," Trey said and started detailing all the logistics of the sale, including the division of assets and the parties involved in the deal. Many times, during his delineation I wanted to ask a question and put the smug asshole on the spot, but held back.

This was Adrian's to handle. I had to trust him. I had a role to play, and so did he. Right now, I was on the stage.

My heart ached for him. He was about to take down his own mother.

Who was I kidding? Adrian was mine. The brother I'd raised.

Trey's voice broke into my thoughts. "As you can see, once you sign, you will be richer than you could ever imagine."

He set a stack of papers in front of me. Was this guy for

real? He really thought I would sign a hundred-page contract without having it reviewed.

I thumbed through the documents and frowned. "This looks nothing like the papers you sent to Carter." I pushed the documents in Trey's direction.

Carter had the same reaction I'd had. "I'm sorry, Mrs. Kipos. I cannot advise my client to sign anything without proper due diligence."

From the corner of my eye, I noticed Dara fidget with her bracelet. It was her first sign she was irritated and on the verge of blowing up. I'd been on the receiving end of it countless times over the years.

"There are a few last-minute revisions. I'm sure a quick review will suffice to satisfy you," Trey said in a sickly sweet, condescending way as if Carter knew nothing about law.

Boy, where had Papa found this guy? I couldn't believe Papa had trusted him for so many years. Well, I guessed, in the end, he hadn't, since he'd hired Carter's father to take over any legal proceedings before his death.

"I'd like to go through it in detail. I won't advise Ms. Kipos to sign anything unless she's completely aware of all changes and clauses."

All of a sudden, Dara shouted in my direction, "I swear, if you don't sign the papers, I will make your life a living hell, Persephone Kipos. I will make it so no one will ever work with you or buy your cheap alcohol."

Fuck this shit. I was not going to let her talk to me like this ever again.

I gave Adrian an apologetic shoulder shrug and stood. "Are you threatening me? I'm not signing anything until I know all the changes you've made. I don't trust you."

"What have I done that is so untrustworthy? I'm not the one who's a whore to three men."

I saw Hagen shift, and I shook my head. This was my fight, as he'd said. He gave me a nod and leaned back in his chair, but there was an edge to the set of his shoulders that told me he'd jump in at any moment if he thought I was in danger.

"Let me make this clear. You need me more than I need you. Without my approval, this deal you have will crumble to dust."

"The only thing I need is your signature," Dara countered, rising to her feet.

"Mother, what are you doing?" Adrian jumped forward but stopped when Trey grabbed Dara's arm and pulled her back down.

"Stay out of this, Adrian. Don't think I don't know that your loyalties are to her. I have reports telling me you spend all your free time with her and at his property." She shot daggers at Hagen, who seemed unfazed. "I'm your mother. Your loyalties are supposed to be to me."

Anger flared in Adrian's eyes, and through gritted teeth, he said, "I am loyal to my mother. She just happens to be my sister, not the woman who gave birth to me."

"You ungrateful boy. Just wait until the money runs out. Don't come crying to me."

"Calm down, Dara." Trey held on to Dara's arm as if he was preparing for her to jump up again. "This session is being recorded as per the board's request."

She jerked her hand free. "I don't give a fuck. I've put up with these brats for too long. Sign the papers, and we can be rid of each other."

"Isn't your sale contingent on the new lucrative contract with PSK Distilleries?" I asked.

All the color drained from Dara's face, and she glanced at Trey. She must have forgotten that I owned PSK and she had to play nice to get what she wanted.

"The details of the deal are privileged information. You are going off of rumors. You know nothing."

"I know a lot of things." I smiled, pulling out my own stack of papers from my shoulder bag. "You see this?" I pushed the documents toward Dara. "This is Papa's last will and testament. The one you conveniently forgot to make public. The one Papa made right before his death. Keeping one's children in the dark about their inheritance is definitely not the actions of a morally superior woman. Wouldn't you agree, Mr. Ritchman?"

Dara remained quiet, trying to mask her shock.

"It is a fraud. Jacob Kipos made no such revised will. I was his legal counsel for over fifteen years." Trey spoke in an angry voice, looking as if he wanted to strangle me.

Yes, asshole. You've been found out.

"I beg to differ, Mr. Ritchman," Carter interjected. "My father was Jacob Kipos's attorney on record at the time of his death. In fact, this will is very valid and filed with the proper channels."

"This means nothing. I'll fight it in court."

"With whose money?" Hagen spoke. "Adrian, don't you have something to show your genetic donor?"

I furrowed my brow. Okay, this was not part of the plan. What the hell was Adrian going to show everyone, and why was Hagen in on it and not me?

I glared at the two men, but they ignored me, keeping their focus on Dara.

"Mother—" Adrian addressed her with a tinge of venom in his voice, "—I have a video to show you. Our friend Josef Petrov gave this to the Lykaioses as payment for the inconvenience your friend Erin Kapok caused them in their hotel. I think you'll find it very interesting. It seems Erin liked to record your time together."

Adrian started the video.

My hands began to shake. It revealed Kapok and Dara making detailed plans on the various ways to get rid of Papa.

I had been right all along.

Oh, Papa. Nausea filled my stomach, and before I knew it, Hagen had me in his arms and was carrying me out of the room and into an empty office.

"I need to see it. I have to see it," I cried as I banged on his chest.

"No, baby, you don't. The authorities will be in there soon to arrest Dara."

"How could you keep this from me? I trusted you."

"It was for your protection."

I couldn't listen to him say that. Protection wasn't letting me walk into a situation like the one that just happened.

"No, dammit. You made the bargain with me, not Adrian. You were supposed to be the one thing in my life that was truly mine. But I was just fooling myself."

"Starlight. Listen to me."

"No." I pushed out of his hold and rushed to the door. "I can't be around any of you right now."

CHAPTER TWENTY

Penny

"COME HERE, BABY GIRL." Amelia Nephus Thanos wrapped her arms around me moments after I landed on the airstrip of her private island an hour off the coast of mainland Greece.

Immediately after I left Kipos headquarters, I called Amelia, giving her a play-by-play of what had happened in my life over the past few weeks. She sent one of her pilots for me, and now a day later I was in Greece. I felt like a wimp for running away, but I couldn't look at either Hagen or Adrian at the moment. They'd conspired to keep me in the dark about Papa's death. Logically I knew their intentions had been to protect me, but I didn't need to be protected all the fucking time.

Adrian had wanted me to trust him, to let him take the lead, but it felt like he hadn't trusted me. And Hagen. He was another story. He had to have known I'd be upset. Maybe I was just fooling myself into thinking there could be more to my relationship with him than sex. I knew he wanted me, but he'd never told me he loved me. Was I fooling myself with the hope there could be more?

I refused to be in a relationship where I wasn't his equal.

"Stop it. I don't think you ran away from your life to brood the whole time you're here." Amelia released me, tucked her arm in mine, and dragged me to a waiting car.

"No, I want to forget for a little while. PSK is covered on the business end, and Ana has the lab handled. So I guess you could say I'm free to do whatever."

A grin touched Amelia's face. "Over the next few days, I'm going to show you how the Widow Thanos spends her days. Maybe after I get your ass into shape, we can give the tabloids something to write about."

"I'm more worried about training than clubbing. You should get me in a cage with one of your prizefighters."

"That's a distinct possibility. Besides, it's good for your health, and you need to set a good example for your godson."

"Speaking of. How is he doing? Did he like his birthday gift from his *Theia* Penny?"

She gave me the side-eye. "Did you really have to send a ten-year-old boy a high-end drum kit? There is nothing but nonstop banging in the house."

"Hey, you should be happy I hired a teacher too. Otherwise, it could be worse."

"True, true."

Penny

"I CAN'T BELIEVE you did this. I would have been fine sitting at your house drinking wine and eating myself into a coma," I said as Amelia and I stepped out of her Mercedes and into the evening heat along the shores of Ibiza, Spain.

"Calm down. It's not like it was around the world. It was a short flight from the island with a ten-minute drive once we landed. And, it's not like we haven't done this before. Besides, I need this as much as you do."

My heart ached for Amelia. In spite of all her talk about tabloids, she was as conservative as they came. And the only person I'd ever known her to let loose with was her deceased husband, Stavros. I'd envied their relationship for so many years. He was the Greek billionaire who'd swept the girl from the world of hard knocks off her feet after her devastating breakup with Pierce.

It wasn't until years later that I learned their marriage had been a deal. Though they had been the best of friends and loved each other dearly, they hadn't been *in* love. Then, after Stavros's unexpected death in a boating accident almost two years ago, Amelia had floundered. Stavros had grounded Amelia, and her anchor was gone.

She'd all but gone into hiding, focusing solely on her son and the business she'd inherited from Stavros.

Only in the last few months had she come back into the world. I had the feeling tonight was as much about her letting loose as it was for me.

We walked up to the club on the beach Amelia had promised was the "it" place to go in Ibiza.

"You have got to be kidding me." I released a sigh as I read the sign of the club. Did everything have to remind me of him? He'd orchestrated everything to keep Dara from winning, but he had no idea that all I wanted was him and to feel his equal.

"What?" Amelia asked. "The *Luz de las Estrellas* is the best club on the island. It means—"

"Starlight," I said, cutting her off.

"Hey, isn't that your middle name?" she said with a twinkle in her eyes.

She knew very well it was my name. "Yes."

Amelia laughed. "It's not so bad. At least you weren't saddled with Moonbeam or something even more hippyish."

"Come on, show me this nightlife Ibiza is known for."

She took my hand and led me straight to a section closed off by ropes. We approached a group of bouncers who smiled at Amelia.

"Hello, Carlos," she said to a big, burly man who looked like a sumo wrestler.

He leaned down, kissing both of Amelia's cheeks. *"Buenas noches, Amelia."*

"We are here for a fun night to forget all our woes. Is my table ready?" she asked in Spanish.

"Of course. I arranged it personally when I heard my manager was coming to see me." He winked.

"Don't think I'll tell Gustav to take it easy on you later this week."

"I wouldn't dare." He smirked and then turned in my direction. *"Who do you have with you..."* He trailed off and then stared at me like I had two heads.

"What? Is there something wrong with me?" I said to Carlos.

"You speak Spanish? I thought you were Indian."

I lifted a brow as if that was a dumb question since my answers were in Spanish. *"Yes, I speak Spanish. And English, Greek, Hindi, and Dutch. I'm a* migas, *as Amelia likes to call me in Greek."*

His cheeks reddened, revealing his embarrassment at his reaction to me.

After a few moments, he shook his head as if to clear his mind, glanced at the other bouncers behind him who seemed as stunned, and then asked, *"Are you alone?"* as he looked behind me, scanning the area.

"Is there a problem?" A twinge of annoyance flared to life.

"No. It's nothing. Please go in." Carlos gestured to the door. *"Go right in."*

I lifted a brow at Amelia, mouthing the words "what the fuck?"

She smirked and shrugged her shoulders. "I have absolutely no idea what the hell that was about."

Why'd I get the feeling she knew exactly what was going on?

"Come on." She pulled me into the crowd of thrashing bodies and rolling hips.

We danced our way through the horde of people intoxicated by the heady energy of music and sex, giving off the very image of what Ibiza was known for. A server stepped in our path as we reached the lounge area, offering us long-stem champagne glasses, and once we took them in our hands, she added a splash of Firewater into them.

"Girl, places like this are making you so rich that you're going to give the Lykaios brothers a run for their money."

Immediately, Amelia realized what she'd said and touched my arm. "I'm sorry, babe. I was trying to keep your mind off him, and here I go mentioning the brothers."

"It's okay." I released a breath and moved toward a group of tables. "The sad part is, if it wasn't for Hagen, I wouldn't have half as much as I currently do."

Now it looked like all the top clubs were following his example and using Firewater as a draw for high-end patrons.

"The world knows you two were an item. Especially after the tabloids posted those recent pictures of you and him walking into the ballroom during the opening at Ida. The photos looked innocent enough, with his arm around your waist, but I have a feeling the flush on your face had a story."

The image of Hagen's mouth on me as I held on to the railing of the balcony caused my core to clench. Thank God, they only got the picture of afterward, not during.

"Who knows if that will happen again. I'm not sure if there is a future there. No matter how much I want one."

"Does he know this? From what I've seen, he looks like a man determined to keep you." Amelia sat down on a long, plush blood-red couch. It was a sharp contrast to the stark white of the club's interior.

"I need more than the intense sex. He's never once said he loves me. Hell, he's never told me how he feels at all about me, and I don't have the time or inclination to wait for him to come to terms with his feelings."

"Liar. You'd wait in hell for him. What you can't handle is not having control of the situation."

"I am not a control freak. I had to learn not to have any while working under Dara at Kipos."

"Speaking of Kipos, what are you going to do with the company?"

"We're selling it. Most of the paperwork is already complete and executed. The next steps are to plan the transitions. In the meantime, we have a team running the company. They're probably the only reason the company has any working capital."

"Let me guess. Hagen found the buyers."

"It was actually Zack."

"Interesting."

"What's that supposed to mean?"

Amelia handed me another drink. "Just think about it. It probably wouldn't have happened if it hadn't been for Hagen. The man is screaming how he feels about you without saying it."

Ignoring the truth of what she said, I drank down half of the glass and glared at Amelia. "I need the words."

"Why, when his actions say it to everyone? You are one of my closest friends, so I'm going to say this. You are a stubborn idiot. Not all men have the ability to say the words. They show it through actions. Hell, the words mean nothing unless there is follow-through."

I closed my eyes.

"Penny, he bent over backward to find out the truth about your Papa. Yeah, he kept you in the dark and then dropped a bombshell on you, but he's a dumb guy. He thought he was protecting you. There is no cure for being a typical man and he will probably fuck up again.

"Forgive him. He stopped your evil stepmother from destroying your father's legacy. He watches after your brother so you don't have to. He designed clubs around a product you created. And most of all, he hasn't really asked for anything in return. Hell, from what you tell me, I think he believes he doesn't deserve you. That man loves you."

I wiped my face as a tear slid down my cheek.

My God. He *had* been saying he loved me. His possessive words were his way of shielding himself from the false belief he wasn't worthy.

I looked up at Amelia's knowing face and said, "I have to go home."

"Spend tonight with me and then I'll have the jet ready for you to leave by eight in the morning."

"Does Christopher know his mom is a hopeless romantic?"

Her smile wavered. "At least one of us gets a happy ending with a Lykaios brother."

"Are you ever going to tell Pierce that Christopher is his son?"

The startled expression she gave me said she hadn't realized I'd figured it out.

"Not if I can help it. I won't taint Stavros's memory."

I nodded.

"How long have you known?"

"Since Christopher was three. You have to remember, I grew up with the brothers. He's an exact copy of Pierce. Well, except the pouty lips. Those are all yours."

Amelia gaped at me. "Why didn't you say anything?"

"Because Stavros was an amazing father and you loved him."

"Thank you." Her lips trembled. "Are you going to tell Hagen?"

"No. I know you have your reasons. Nothing's simple when it comes to the Lykaios brothers. Besides, you're my ride or die, and we've always kept each other's secrets."

"Isn't that the truth?" She picked up her drink, downing it in a few swallows.

I decided it was time to change the subject and stood, offering Amelia my hand. "Let's go. Time to shake our tail feathers."

Amelia set her glass on the table and rose. Before we could get out of the lounge area, a gorgeous Adonis walked up to Amelia and asked her to dance. She gave him a bright smile and nodded. Within seconds, she disappeared into the crowd.

I made my way to the dance floor. I caught a glimpse of Amelia. She laughed at something the guy said, with the melancholy of a few minutes ago gone.

I had a feeling she'd have to deal with an avalanche of chaos when Pierce found out about Christopher, but at least she could let her hair down now.

Taking my cue from her, I engulfed myself in the music and began to dance. There were too many people to feel alone. The problem was that everywhere I looked something would remind me of Hagen. From the serpent patterns around the columns of the club that resembled the one etched on Hagen's arm to the white decor splashed with red, giving the illusion of fire.

Hagen was everything this club represented, high end, indulgence, and a heady mix of sex.

Sadness filled my heart. I could still see the resignation in his eyes when I'd left. He'd done all of it for me, and I hadn't wanted to see past the shock of what had happened.

Amelia was right. He'd been telling me over and over how he felt, and I'd ignored it. In a few hours, I'd leave and try to fix this. I could only imagine how hurt he must have been when he discovered I'd disappeared. He'd probably tried to tear Vegas apart, especially since I hadn't let any of my girls know I was leaving.

Oh well, I couldn't do anything about it now.

I scanned the club, watching all the beautiful people of Ibiza enjoying the nightlife. It was an eclectic mix of people dancing, laughing, and enjoying the celebrity DJ's mixes.

An attractive blond with the physique of one of Amelia's fighters came up to me and began to dance. I glanced in her direction. She gave me a big smile, and I knew she'd sent this handsome man in my direction.

I hesitated for a second and then I decided to enjoy myself. It wasn't as if I planned to go home with him. It was just a dance. Hagen couldn't possibly get jealous of a dance.

Who was I kidding? Hagen would probably lose his mind if he found out about this, but then again, who was going to tell him?

I stepped toward the guy and offered my hand. "I'm Penny."

"I'm David. Amelia said you'd enjoy some company."

That was the extent of our discussion as the music changed to a unique mix of trance, hip-hop, and EDM.

He pulled me toward him. I almost hesitated but then decided I could let go for a few minutes. We began to dance, and I gave myself up to the grinding rhythm.

By the end of two sets, I was dripping in sweat from the summer heat and the exertion of the dancing. I decided to take a break. There was only so long I could pretend it was Hagen who held me and moved against my body. Though the energy around me made me feel like he was there.

Pulling free of David, I turned and slammed straight into a broad chest I was very intimately familiar with.

That explained the way I was feeling. Any time this man was in the vicinity, I was hornier than a teenager.

The look in his eyes told me I was in deep shit.

He slid one hand into my sweat-soaked hair, fisting it in a tight grip, and the other around my waist, pulling me against him.

"What are you doing here?" I asked a bit too breathlessly.

He ignored my question as he began to move our bodies to the rhythm of the next set the DJ mixed. I gripped his shoulders, meeting the demand of his hips by rolling my pelvis to his rhythm.

Arousal began to tingle through my body, making my

nipples bead into hard, sensitized peaks. Dammit, the slightest graze of his body made me want to beg him to fuck me.

After we danced for a few minutes, he bit my earlobe and said, "You let another man touch what's mine."

"It was one dance." My fingers crept up behind his neck, and I leaned in, inhaling the crisp, clean scent of him.

God, he smelled good.

He tugged my head back and glared down. "No, it was two."

"Are you stalking me?"

"Yes." His hold in my hair tightened. "You left me. You didn't even let me know you were leaving the country. I was fucking out of my mind."

The fact he'd come after me wasn't lost on me.

"You pissed me off. I may let you control the show in the bedroom, but that's where it ends."

"Is that right?" He ground his thick, hard cock against my clit as we danced, sending a wave of desperate need to my aching pussy.

A moan escaped my lips before I could hold it back.

A wicked smile touched his mouth, and it gave me the urge to deck him. He knew how he affected me and had no issues using it to his advantage. I tried to pull out of his hold, but he wouldn't budge.

"You agreed to play with the devil, Starlight. Now he owns you."

"What about me? Do I own you?"

He held my gaze, and a war of emotions passed in his blue depths. "There hasn't been a time that you haven't owned me."

My heart skipped a beat. I wanted so desperately for him to tell me how he felt about me, and now, here he was.

I cupped his cheek and lifted onto my toes, kissing him in the middle of the dance floor, not caring that cameras and anyone with a cell phone could capture the moment and possibly plaster it on all the tabloids.

"What have you done to me?" he murmured against my lips.

"Nothing you haven't done to me."

He pulled back, looking me up and down. "That skirt is indecent."

I shrugged and turned, rubbing my behind against his hard length.

One of his hands slid around my bare midriff as the other glided up my stomach, between the valley of my breasts, and around my throat. Tilting my head up, I stared into his blue gaze and then met his mouth as it came down on mine again.

"I love you," I murmured against his lips.

He closed his eyes for a brief moment. "Just so we're

clear. I don't care if you are pissed to holy hell at me. I'm never letting you go. You're mine forever."

"What if I said I don't want you to let me go?"

"I find that acceptable," he said into my hair. "But there is one thing I need to do at this moment."

"What's that?"

"I need to fuck you."

CHAPTER TWENTY-ONE

Hagen

"WHAT IF I said I don't want you to let me go?"

Starlight's words echoed in my head as I held her hand and weaved through the body-to-body crowd. My need for her was a violent mix of desire and anger. If she didn't want me to let her go, then why'd she leave?

I'd nearly gone out of my mind when I discovered she hadn't even told Adrian where she was going. If it hadn't been for a call from Collin telling me one of his men had seen the chartered plane she'd boarded, I would have no idea where she was.

The man was determined to fix our relationship, and

some part of me wanted to. It would take time to repair the damage he'd done, but the door was open.

That was neither here nor there. At this moment, I wanted to fuck Starlight until she felt me with every step she took and craved me as much as I craved her.

As I approached a set of doors leading to the VIP areas of the club, the group of bouncers guarding the area straightened and stared between Starlight and me.

"She's real?" one said in amazement and a little too much excitement.

It took all my will not to clock the idiot. Instead, I glared at him.

He flinched and then said, "Sorry, boss. I mean, Mr. Lykaios."

The bouncer moved to the side.

"What was that about? Boss? Don't tell me you own this place too. I guess the Lykaios brothers have their hands in international indulgences in addition to their domination of Vegas. I should have guessed with the club's name."

I kept quiet, guiding her toward the club offices. She'd find out soon enough my obsession with the woman I never expected to have.

"Are you ignoring me, boss?"

I scowled at her over my shoulder. "Explanations later.

At this moment all I want to think about is my cock buried deep in your cunt."

"I have no problem with that." A flush covered her face, and the puckering of her nipples grew harder.

The second we entered the VIP lounge, Starlight abruptly stopped.

Her gaze was fixed on a collage of images featuring supermodels, celebrities, high-end clientele, and in the center of them was a picture of her.

She was staring into the distance stirring a drink with a bottle of Firewater in front of her. She was sitting at a bar with one of her Indian distilleries in the background. She wore a loose-fitting shirt and a hat to shade her from the blazing sun in India. There wasn't a stitch of makeup on her breathtaking face, revealing the natural beauty she was blessed with.

It was my all-time favorite picture of her. She looked like a supermodel in an ad campaign for her whiskey, but it was a candid, unposed shot.

She'd think I was crazy if she knew how many times I'd jacked off to a vision of her getting up from the image, walking up to me, and then dropping to her knees to suck me off.

She turned to me, and I couldn't help but feel a twinge of apprehension. "So I guess I know how you found out my secret."

I kept quiet, not sure what to say.

"Did you have me followed?"

I shook my head as my hands came instinctively around her waist, pulling her toward me.

I leaned my forehead against hers and decided to give her the details. "I found out by accident. I didn't have you followed. One of my researchers was on vacation in India and decided to visit a local pub. He noticed a beautiful local woman that he couldn't keep his eyes off of and took a few pictures. It wasn't until later when he looked at them that he realized it was you. So he sent me one of the pictures." I gestured to the one on the wall. "I confirmed it was you and then noticed the bottle on the table."

"That picture was three years ago."

"Yes."

"How old is this club?"

"A little over two years."

"So you named the club after me."

It wasn't a question, but I responded anyway. "Yes."

A wicked look passed in her gaze and she lifted onto her toes, gripping me behind my head, and peered at me. "How long have you been in love with me?"

"Starlight." Her name came out rougher than I intended. How could I tell her that what I felt for her went beyond love? She wanted to know what she meant to me, but there were no words to describe it.

The flight over had convinced me I wouldn't be able to live without her. I'd give her the words if it meant she stayed, but the closer I got to Spain, I knew I wouldn't hold her to me, no matter what I said. All I could do was tell her what she meant to me and hope she accepted. Then I saw her dancing with that fucker, and all I could see was red.

Now here she was waiting for an answer, and I was tongue-tied.

"I don't think there was a time I haven't loved you," I said in a rush, feeling a bit dizzy.

Tears filled her green gaze. "Now was that so hard?"

She buried her face against my chest as her hands wrapped around my waist.

"You have no idea." I cradled her against me.

"Well, there's a first time for everything."

I lifted her chin to look up at me. "You're telling me. I've never chased a woman before. You bring out a side of me that I never knew existed."

"Zack says I make you insane because you can't compartmentalize me. I like that."

"Zack talks too much," I muttered, but couldn't be angry with him since my Starlight was smiling at me. "I don't know where to go from here, Starlight."

"I suggest home."

"Where is home? Your family house? It belongs to you and Adrian, free and clear."

"No, it's a penthouse in the clouds that overlooks the Strip. There's a Master of Sin who lives there that I can't get enough of."

My fingers flexed. "Are you sure you want to go there? You may never get to leave. Plus, he'll probably corrupt your innocence."

"Too late. I already belong to him. He owns me. And you know what?"

"What?"

"I own him."

I leaned down to kiss her. "That you do. That you do."

The End

NOTE FROM THE AUTHOR:

Word-of-mouth is an important tool for every author. If you enjoyed this book, please review this book online. Even if it is one or two sentences, it would make a difference and I'd greatly appreciate it.

Follow the link and pick your preferred retailer to review -> Books2Read.com/MasterOfSin

Much love,
Sienna

Read the next book in the Gods of Vegas Series.

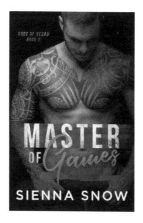

May 8, 2019

Preorder now → books2read.com/MasterofGames

***He was my obsession. Haunting my dreams,
reminding me of my past.***

He was the one whose heart I destroyed.

Pierce Lykaios was everything I could want: captivating,
cunning, and controlled. He understood my darkest desires
and took pleasure in feeding my every craving.

And when I walked back into his world, it was my fault for
letting the first touch lead to a second. And a third. I
shouldn't have let him reawaken my need.

Now I'm caught in his grasp with no hope of escape,
unable to forget, unable to stop.

He says this time I won't leave him. I won't forget him.

And I'm afraid he's right.

ABOUT THE AUTHOR

Inspired by her years working in corporate America, Sienna loves to serve up stories woven around confident and successful women who know what they want and how to get it, both in – and out – of the bedroom.

Her heroines are fresh, well-educated, and often find love and romance through atypical circumstances. Sienna treats her readers to enticing slices of hot romance infused with empowerment and indulgent satisfaction.

Sienna loves the life of travel and adventure. She plans to visit even the farthest corners of the world and delight in experiencing the variety of cultures along the way. When she isn't writing or traveling, Sienna is working on her "happily ever after" with her husband and children.

Sign up for her newsletter to be notified of releases, book sales, events and so much more.

www.SiennaSnow.com

facebook.com/authorsiennasnow

instagram.com/bysiennasnow

twitter.com/sienna_snow

BOOKS BY SIENNA SNOW

Rules of Engagement

Rule Breaker

Rule Master

Rule Changer

Politics of Love

Celebrity

Senator

Commander

Gods of Vegas

Master of Sin

Master of Games (May 2019)

Master of Revenge (July 2019)

Master of Secrets (September 2019)

Made in the USA
Middletown, DE
16 April 2022